D0465465

THE
UNFORTUNATES

ALSO BY KIM LIGGETT

The Last Harvest

THE UNFORTUNATES

KIM LIGGETT

TOR TEEN

A TOM DOHERTY ASSOCIATES BOOK / NEW YORK

THE UNFORTUNATES

Copyright © 2018 by Kim Liggett

A Tor Teen Book
Published by Tom Doherty Associates
175 Fifth Avenue
New York, NY 10010

www.tor-forge.com

Tor® is a registered trademark of Macmillan Publishing Group, LLC.

The Library of Congress Cataloging-in-Publication Data is available upon request.

ISBN 978-0-7653-8100-2 (hardcover)
ISBN 978-1-4668-7631-6 (ebook)

Our books may be purchased in bulk for promotional, educational, or business use. Please contact your local bookseller or the Macmillan Corporate and Premium Sales Department at 1-800-221-7945, extension 5442, or by email at MacmillanSpecialMarkets@macmillan.com.

First Edition: July 2018

Printed in the United States of America

0 9 8 7 6 5 4 3 2

33614081600461

Beware that, when fighting monsters, you yourself do not become a monster . . . for when you gaze long into the abyss, the abyss gazes also into you.

—FRIEDRICH NIETZSCHE

THE
UNFORTUNATES

1

"GRANT Franklin Tavish the fifth?" the burly nurse calls into the waiting room.

Everyone around me bursts out laughing.

"That's gotta be this kid." The guy across from me leans back in the bright-orange molded-plastic chair, spreading his legs farther than I thought humanly possible.

"What'd you do?" The old man next to me nudges my elbow. "Get caught sneaking into your daddy's liquor cabinet? Smoke a little weed under the bleachers?"

I let out an exasperated sigh, like this is the worst day of my life, but the truth is, I like it here. For twenty minutes a week, I get to live in reality. This is where I belong.

Somewhere worse really, but things like that don't happen to Tavishes.

As I'm walking toward the door with a tiny window lined with security wire, a guy from the far side of the room says, "Hey, wait a minute. I know you . . ."

I pause, waiting for him to say it. Aching for him to call me out for what I really am.

"Aren't you the senator's son . . . the one from the news? The one who—"

"That's enough," the nurse says, ushering me through the door. "He's here . . . just the same as you clowns."

I follow him down the dingy hall, which reeks of piss and bleach, to door number three. There's a metal sink, metal toilet, metal walls. The fluorescent lights ping as if in the throes of death.

"You know the drill," the nurse says as he makes note of the time and the serial number off the plastic cup before handing it over.

Unbuckling my belt, I drop my khakis and boxers to my ankles and pull up my dress shirt and tie. It's humiliating, but that's kind of the whole point.

"Hope you drank your fresh-squeezed OJ this morning," he says as he snaps on a pair of latex gloves. "I can't be standing here for ten minutes singing you 'Tinkle, Tinkle, Little Star.'"

I roll back my shoulders, trying to relax.

The first time I came in here it took me six minutes to even squeeze out a drop. They made me go back to the waiting room and drink a liter of water before they let me try again. But I've been practicing at home. I realize how ridiculous that sounds. Even taking a drug test, I have to strive to be the best. It's ingrained.

I close my eyes, thinking of class three rapids, rain pouring out of the copper gutters outside my bedroom window, the surf hitting the sand at our beach house—but then the sound of screeching tires and hot oil dripping onto freezing pavement slips over my senses.

"You don't remember anything," our lawyer whispers in my ear.

"Think we've got enough," the nurse says, staring down at the overflowing cup.

"Sorry." I flinch, sloshing it over the sides.

He takes it from me, secures the lid, and unlocks the tiny metal door in the wall, sliding it through.

"I wonder what happens to all those plastic cups," I say, trying to shake off the memory. "Maybe in a few hundred years they'll dig it up, think it's some precious family heirloom."

He looks up at me with one raised eyebrow. "You think too much, kid."

If he only knew.

As I'm washing my hands, he flips through my chart. "I see this is your last time." He juts out his bottom lip and bobs his head. "Final court date on Monday. If this comes back negative, you get a clean slate."

"Best justice money can buy," I mutter as I put my hands under the wheezing dryer.

"What was that?"

"Nothing," I say as I straighten my tie in the smudged book-size mirror.

I want to tell him there's nothing about my slate that could ever be clean, not after what I did, but I can't risk it. Not now. Not when I'm this close.

Instead, I crack a smile. The one that says, *Don't worry. I'm all good now.*

The one I've practiced to perfection.

2

THE walk from the ugly, squat redbrick building to the awaiting black sedan feels like I'm trudging against a strong current. Sometimes I wonder if you can see it on me. If someone took my photo, would it show up on the negative? The death hanging all around me?

"Don't dawdle," my mother says as I open the door.

She's in the back, perched on the edge of the seat, probably applying her tenth coat of nude lipstick. It's her tic, what she does when she's uncomfortable. I don't get nude lipstick. If you're going to wear the same shade as your lips, what's the point? But I don't feel like provoking her. Not today.

It seems funny to me that I have no idea what she looks

like without makeup, without the expensive dress suits. I wonder if I'd even recognize her in holey sweats and a T-shirt, her perfect bob pulled into some dirty scrunchie. The thought makes me laugh.

"You find this amusing?" She snaps her compact shut. "I'll never understand why you insisted on taking care of this downtown. Dr. Wilson would've been more than happy to collect it from the house. I'm sure the judge would've–"

"I think we've asked enough favors." I settle back in my seat. "Besides, this is nothing compared to–"

"I'm fully aware." She cuts me off, clutching her purse tight to her chest as some guy in an oversize army surplus coat approaches the car, staring into the tinted windows. "Can we go now, please?" my mother asks, her voice tighter than the lid of my piss cup.

Without a word, Marvin slowly pulls the car out of the lot.

I catch his eyes in the rearview mirror. I wonder what he thinks of us. What he tells his family when he goes home at night. If he even has a family. He's been driving my mother around for the past couple of years. He probably knows her better than any of us. I rarely see them speak, but he seems to anticipate her every need. Little things, like handing her a tissue before she even sneezes. Knowing if she's hot or cold.

My mother demands excellence from everyone around her, but she holds herself to the same standard, so it's hard not to respect that. People think my dad's the one with all the power, but it's really her, pulling the strings. She would've been an amazing politician. Sharp. Strategic. Ambitious. I can't imagine how frustrating that must've been for her—saddled with three kids, losing one, stifling all that unmet potential in order to help my father's star rise, to help us become all the things she never had the opportunity to be. But behind that pleasant smile, she's a force to be reckoned with. When I was a kid, I used to wonder if she was even human.

"Marvin will pick you up after school. I understand you have a few errands, but I need you home as soon as possible for your portrait sitting. I'll be tied up with the photographer from *Richmond Life*. They're coming out to the house to capture the tulips. Family dinner is at seven thirty sharp. Your father will want to go over the plans for your trip, so you should . . ."

I smile. Nod on cue. But I've completely tuned her out now. Most people avoid silence because it leaves them with their thoughts. I used to be like that. But I don't want to forget what happened. I don't deserve that kind of peace.

After the "incident," when my mother came to the hospital, her eyes full of tears, she leaned over and hugged me. I couldn't remember the last time that happened. I wrapped my arms around her and wept like a baby. All I needed in that moment was to feel loved . . . to feel safe . . . to be forgiven.

But then she whispered in my ear . . .

Not *I love you.*

Not *I'm glad that you're okay.*

She whispered, "How could you do this to me?"

To *me*.

It felt like a sucker punch. Even thinking about it now brings that sour taste to the back of my throat. I'd never felt so despised in all my life.

In my mother's eyes, it's like we're all just props to be moved around as she sees fit. And I went off script, in the biggest way possible. Sometimes I wonder if it would've been easier for her if I'd just died that night. She's never said as much, but I feel it every time she looks at me.

The thing is, I know she loves me. I know she only wants what she believes is best for me. But she doesn't have a clue. All she wants to do is bury it, like she buries everything else. It's kind of ironic that it took all this to make me realize she's just a human being.

Without thinking, I reach over the divider and take her hand in mine, squeezing tight.

She's so caught off guard that she stammers. I've never heard my mother stammer before.

"W-well . . . how nice." She quickly pulls her hand out from under mine and gives it a pat before applying another coat of nude lipstick.

3

AS soon as we pull up to St. Augustine, I get out as quickly as possible. It's not that I'm embarrassed my mother has to take me to school—I'm well beyond that now—and I'm more than happy to be rid of the bodyguards. It's just that sometimes, ever since the "incident," when I'm in a confined space like that, it feels like I can't breathe . . . like I'm choking under the weight of it all.

I see a flash in my peripheral, nothing more than a passing shadow, but it gets my full attention. It's been months, the media has surely moved on by now, but lately I've had the distinct feeling that I'm being followed, watched. Sometimes I even hear a whisper. As I stare into the parking lot, I quiet myself, listen closely, and then quickly realize how insane this is. I know I'm probably just being paranoid, but I can't afford to have any interference at this point.

"Hey! Grant!" Bennett and Parker flag me over.

As I walk across the impossibly green lawn, watching them hold court, I can't believe I was ever one of them. Three months ago, we were all inseparable, and now they seem like an entirely different species.

They're not bad people. I mean, they do their Habitat for Humanity vacations, drink free-trade coffee, go to Christ Episcopal on Sundays—all the things people like us are supposed to do. They could've easily frozen me out after the incident, but that's not how we're raised. These are the same people I'm expected to build my entire future around. There will be golf trips, duck hunting trips, vacations with our wives, where we can all pretend we're still in high school and reminisce about how these were the best years of our lives . . . until eventually we believe it.

It's pounded into us from birth that the kids you come up with—from prep school, camp, lacrosse, college—those are your people. The only ones you can trust. They don't need money. They don't need a leg up. They're from the same families who've held on to their wealth through wars, depression, the collapse of industry. In Richmond, we stick to our own and close ranks when things get sticky. But it's more than that. I think they know it could've been any one of them that night.

But it wasn't.

It was me.

"Are you pumped for break?" Parker passes me the Hacky Sack. I kick it back on pure instinct. "Sally's parents are in Europe." He grins. "It's going to be sick."

"Can't," I say as I set down my bag and pull on my blazer. "I've got the trail this week. Four nights. I'm leaving tomorrow, coming back Sunday."

"You're still doing that?" Bennett winces. "I thought . . ."

"You thought what?" I ask, eager for even a glimmer of honesty, a moment of recognition for what happened.

"No . . . I just . . . That's not really your thing." He shrugs, trying to keep it casual, but I can tell he's worried. "I didn't think your dad was still making you do that . . . that you'd be up for it."

"Come on." Parker clamps his hand over my shoulder. "Of course he's up for it. It's a Tavish tradition. Man against the elements. Time to get on with life, right?"

I look down at his hand on my shoulder, his signet ring glistening in the bright morning sun, and I want to knock it off, but I can't. I just have to hold it together for a little longer. "Right," I answer through clenched teeth.

"It's better than my old man," Parker says with a forced laugh. "He's obsessed with me pledging Skulls. Legacy. What are you going to do."

"I don't know. What *are* you going to do?" Bennett replies, completely deadpan.

"You're just jealous." Parker shakes his head. "You wouldn't be riding me if you saw the girls they get over there."

Bennett's eyes flash toward me, but I pretend not to notice. "I have one word for you," he says as he checks his cuff links. "Hazing. Have fun getting your balls shaved by a bunch of posers."

"Shut up." Parker beams the Hacky Sack at him.

But I can tell by the way he's laughing, the way the tips of his ears are turning red, that he's secretly jonesing for it. He can't wait to have his balls shaved by a bunch of posers, because that's what his dad did, and his dad before that. He's been preparing for this moment his whole life.

Catherine walks across campus with Lewis. She's holding his hand, smiling up at him, just like she used to with me, but I can see the tension in her neck, the vein that always gives her away.

It reminds me of our first day back after Christmas break, after the incident. She picked me up and, instead of talking about what happened, seeing if I was okay, she turned up the stereo, singing along to her favorite Taylor Swift song. Which was apparently our song. As we pulled in the lot, she smoothed her hair down and touched up her lipstick—just like my mother.

And that's when it hit me. Getting out of the car with me, smiling, holding my hand—this was damage control. Plain and simple.

I'd seen my parents do it a number of times. Like when my dad's name surfaced on that call girl's list, they marched hand in hand from the front door to the gates, presenting a united front as the cameras flashed all around them. And I suppose I could've easily played my dad's role—poured all of my attention into her, the humbled man—but I couldn't do that to her. I couldn't do that to me.

As they stand at the edge of the brick courtyard, I watch her bouncing on the tips of her toes a few times, all to draw the eye, that hundred-watt smile, meant to make you feel like you're looking into the sun. I see through all that now. I wonder if she even knows she's doing it or if it's just part of her DNA.

It's funny how you think you know someone, but all I really know about her are the adorable little things she wanted me to know. I'm not saying it was all fake. We had our moments. And I care about her. I genuinely want her to be happy. But I think Catherine loved the *idea* of me—the name, the life we'd share, our three kids, the lab. She probably had our lives planned since Cotillion. We'd both go to GW, get married right after college, get a brownstone in Arlington. I'd work in the capital, she'd help me climb the political ladder. She never asked me what I wanted. No one did. But to be fair, I never told them, either. I was just as caught up in all this as the rest of them.

Looking at her now with Lewis, it makes me realize how interchangeable I was—all of us, really. Old money, Social Register, Greenbrier at Christmas, summers on the shore. We're all just carbon copies of our parents. And, for the life of me, I can't figure out why we were in such a hurry to step into their shoes.

As soon as she lets go of Lewis's hand and starts walking over, I look away, but it's too late.

"Incoming." Bennett nudges me.

I can feel everyone staring, waiting for some kind of drama, but they're wasting their energy.

"Can I talk to you for a sec?" Catherine asks, tucking a silky strand of honey-colored hair behind her ear.

"Sure," I say as I reluctantly pull away from the group.

When everyone's out of earshot, she says, "I just want to make sure you're okay with this."

"With what?" I put my hands in my pockets. Hands give away so much.

"Me . . . and Lewis." She glances back at him, standing there like a nob, holding her purse. "It just kind of happened."

I know exactly how it just kind of happened, but the last thing I want to do is embarrass her.

"I think it's perfect."

"Perfect?" A tight smile stretches across her glossy pink lips.

"That you found each other." I look off toward the woods, wishing I were anywhere but here, in this moment.

"Well, I guess that's it then," she says as she plays with the pearl on her necklace, the one my mother picked out for her sweet sixteen.

I start to walk away, but when I think about the trail trip, what this means, I turn back. "You know it's not your fault, right?"

Flustered by my break in protocol, she blurts, "I

would've stood by you. No matter what. I wanted to, but–"

"We're all good." I nod. "It's time to . . . move on."

That phrase usually infuriates me. But this time I mean it.

4

BEFORE final bell is even finished ringing, I'm out the door, sprinting across campus, waving at people, pretending I have somewhere important to be, but really I just don't want to talk to anyone. I've said everything I need to say.

I spot my mother's car toward the front of the carpool line and get in, sinking into the dark interior. Taking off my jacket and tie, I fold them into my bag and roll up my sleeves. The cool leather feels good against my clammy skin. I used to make fun of my parents for having tinted windows, but I'm grateful for it now. It's exhausting having to wear a mask all day. I know most people probably look at me and think I have it made. That I got off easy because of my dad. But I don't feel like a prince of Virginia anymore. I feel like an imposter. Like any day they're going to peel back my skin and see the monster that I really am.

"Where to, Mr. Tavish?"

"Please, call me Grant," I say.

Marvin nods and smiles, but I know he won't do it. He's old-school like that.

"Outdoor World. I have to pick up some gear for my trip. But you can just drop me off. I'm meeting a friend there."

"Mrs. Tavish was very specific—"

"I'm sure she was," I say with a lighthearted laugh.

He doesn't say anything, but I can tell by the glint in his eyes that he knows exactly what I'm talking about. She must be a handful. I feel bad doing this to Marvin. The last thing I want to do is get him in trouble, but I need space . . . I need air. I just want to walk home, clear my head before tomorrow.

"All right, Mr. Tavish," he says as he pulls out of the circular drive. "But if there's any trouble, I want you to call me."

As he takes a left on Grace Street, I realize he's taking the long way around. My mother must've told him to avoid going anywhere near Cherokee Drive—the vicinity of the incident. My parents have gone to great lengths to keep me away from it all. No TV, no internet. But I heard the term *affluenza* being thrown around. I knew there were death threats. For the first six weeks, I had security following me, watching my every move, but when I told my parents that it was drawing unnecessary attention to me, to the family, they pulled back. A couple of strange things have happened—random people taking my photo, a few crazies screaming at me about the end of days—but it's mostly a feeling. I realize that sounds delusional, but when you live in a vacuum like this, your mind can play tricks on you.

The reality is no one talked about it. I never had to face the families, hear about their lives. Sometimes it makes me wonder if it ever happened at all. But when Monday rolls around, my one and only court appearance, it will be unavoidable. I wonder what hearing someone speak it aloud would feel like. A relief, I imagine. Painful relief. Like taking a thick, deep splinter from beneath your nail. I've been instructed by my father's lawyer to say four words. Nothing more. Nothing less. *I don't remember anything.* Say the magic words and all of this will go away. My record will be expunged and soon it will be nothing but a distant memory . . . a long-forgotten nightmare. But the more they try to bury it, the more it grows inside of me. Like it's eating me from the inside out.

"Just follow your heart," Marvin says.

"Sorry?" I lean forward, wondering if I missed something.

"Best cure for whatever's worrying you. Follow your heart. I know it sounds simple, but it's always worked for me. I know you'll do the right thing."

His words hit me with brute force, knocking the wind right out of me.

As soon as he turns in to the parking lot, I open my door. "Thanks for everything," I call out as I escape the car, making a beeline for the store. As much as I try to force the air in and out of my lungs, my body rejects it. The pavement in front of me seems to stretch out for miles; there's a high ringing noise flooding my eardrums, hot acid burning the back of my throat. I stagger to the side of the building, by the Dumpsters, and get sick. I haven't eaten today, so it feels like I'm wrenching up pure poison. Bracing my hands against the cool brick wall, I slowly regain my equilibrium. I look back to make sure no one saw me, and I get that feeling again.

I spot my mother's car pulling back onto Lassiter Road.

If it's Marvin who's been watching me all this time, does he know the truth? I start replaying every interaction I've had with him over the past three months, but nothing sticks out. I've been so careful. No. He's probably just making conversation.

The *right thing*.

If only it were that simple.

Either I betray my family or I betray myself. Those were the options that were given to me.

But I have a plan of my own.

5

AS I enter the store, I'm hit with a burst of pine. They must pump it through the ventilation system to make it feel manlier in here. Whatever the reason, I'm grateful. Anything to dull the stench of bile.

Grabbing a basket, I walk through the aisles. I pick up some rope, bolt anchors, a handful of carabiners, but my attention is elsewhere. A couple of guys offer to help, but they're not what I'm looking for. I need someone younger, talkative. But more importantly, I need to make sure I'm in a good position, where the hidden security cameras can get a clean shot.

I spot a guy with the beginnings of a man bun, plaid

shirt, jeans rolled up a little too high to show off his Wallabees. He's perfect.

Milling around, I wait until he's done with a customer and then drop a carabiner out of my basket.

"I love that old Prusik model," he says. "Very trustworthy."

"Good to know," I reply as I pick it up.

"Gearing up for a trip?"

"Yeah. I'm going to start at Crystal Falls, descend Widow's Peak, and then I'm going to camp on the trail for a few days."

"Are you doing your ascent at Custer's Chimney?"

"That's the plan. Have you done it?"

"No, but I'm jealous. I've heard it's killer. Are you going with the school group?"

"No. It's a solo trip . . . before graduation. It's tradition in my family. Kind of a rite of passage, I guess."

"Now I'm super jealous." He steps toward me. "Are you a caver?"

"First time, but I took a course."

"Here at the store?"

"Online. I'm pretty good on the climbing wall though," I say as I look back toward the kids grunting their way to the top. "How different can it be, right?"

"Well . . ." He looks in my basket. "You're definitely going to need a headlamp."

I follow him to the next aisle, where he picks up a helmet with a light attached.

"No helmet," I say, a little too forcefully, and then quickly dial it back. "I'm just not really into them."

"I'm the same," he admits sheepishly. "It's the constriction of movement that bugs me." He picks up another one. "How about something like this?" He shows me a headband with a light on the front. "Newest technology. LED. This will last you fifty thousand hours."

"Is that the strongest battery available?"

He raises a brow. "That's about six years of continuous light. How long is your trip again?"

"No, no . . . it's only four days. I was just curious."

"Oh, you had me nervous there for a second. You wouldn't be the first, you know," he says as he looks around before continuing. "Plenty of people go down there just to live. Survivalists . . . fugitives. Did you read about that one guy, been living down there for seventeen years? Serial killer. I think he murdered like nine people down there, just for fun. Can you imagine?"

Feeling flustered, I grab the headlamp from him. "Thanks. I think this will do it."

"Hey!"

I turn, waiting for the inevitable *Aren't you the senator's son?*, but instead he says, "Aren't you forgetting something?"

I look in my basket, puzzled by where he's going with this.

"Ascent gear. You've got everything for the drop, and nothing to get back out."

"Yeah." I force a laugh. "I've got some gear at home,

but I might as well pick up the newest stuff. You can never be too careful." I feel like I'm babbling now.

Just shut up.

"This is a great Z-rig. I use this one myself," he says as he hands me the pulley rack. "Hey, I hope I didn't scare you with the whole serial killer thing. That was way down in that cave system . . . not even close to where you're going–"

"No . . . not at all."

Clearly, he has no idea who he's dealing with.

"But definitely watch out for that flowstone near Widow's Peak; I heard it can get slick."

"Got it. Thanks."

As I'm checking out, I'm going over the conversation in my head, hoping I didn't screw up too bad. But it's done. I can't get a redo.

That's something I've had to learn the hard way.

6

THE walk home is exactly what I need. I take back roads so I won't raise too much attention. I know it's risky being out in the open like this, especially with the death threats, but that's the least of my problems right now. I need time to pull myself together, go over everything in my head. Tonight has to be perfect. I've already caused them enough grief.

As I'm coming up Windsor, toward Cary Street, I see a dog running down the middle of the road with his tail down. As I get closer, I realize it's Duke.

"Hey, buddy," I call to him. "What're you doing out here?"

I go to grab him by the collar, only to find it's missing. He nuzzles into my leg, whining as he looks behind him.

And that's when I notice the man standing in the street. At least, I think it's a man. It's too dark to make out the face, but I see Duke's collar dangling in the person's hand, the tags glinting in the dying light. I think I hear whispering, but I can't make out the words.

"Who's there?" I call.

I reach down to grab my phone out of my bag, and by the time I look up, they're gone, the collar lying there on the pavement.

Letting out a huge gust of air, I pull my hair back from my face. I'm not sure if there really was someone standing there or if it's my paranoia kicking in, but it doesn't matter at this point. Even if there is someone after me, they're too late.

I put Duke's collar back on him and lead him back to the house. "I don't know how you got out, bud, but we're going to keep this between us." The last thing I need is for my parents to get spooked and put me back under surveillance.

As I'm putting the code in the gate, my sister's voice booms through the intercom.

"You're in so much trouble."

A ripple of panic rushes through me. "Why?" I ask as the gate opens and I shoo Duke through.

"You missed your portrait sitting."

"Oh." I exhale, relieved to find my secrets are still safe. "You could've taken my place, you know."

33

"I'm just a girl, Grant. I don't get a portrait until I'm in my wedding gown."

"That's so archaic." I'm squinting into the camera, trying to fix my hair, when my sister comes back on.

"And you better put on your jacket and tie. Mom's on a level seven tonight."

I look at my watch. 7:28. Two minutes until dinner.

"And I'd really like to keep her below a nine, so you better run."

I sprint down the long drive, putting on my jacket and tie on the way. Duke's chasing after me, barking at nothing but my shadow, and for a brief minute I feel okay again, like all of this is just some big misunderstanding. Somehow we've gone back to Thanksgiving break, when I had nothing on my mind other than finals, going skiing, maybe getting laid. But then I remember what I did, and the feeling comes flooding back to me. That pit in my stomach opens up, instantly filling with bile and guilt.

I open the front door just as my sister's coming down the stairs. Mare and I look almost exactly alike, except for the obvious differences. She's two years younger than me, but people think we're twins. I used to hate it, but it doesn't bother me anymore.

Mare plays the game with my parents, her friends, but she's different than the rest of them. She doesn't have a selfish bone in her body. I've seen her help people—total strangers—not just to put on a college application, not for any kind of recognition, but just because she's decent like that. She's always had this independent streak that I really admire, but lately I've noticed a change in her. Pushing her food around her plate, like Mom. Straightening her hair like all the other sheep. There's this boarding school out West that she's been dying to go to for years. It's all about the arts and activism, but my parents have shot her down at every pass. Now she doesn't even ask anymore. I don't know if it's because of what happened to me or just a part of growing up, but it feels like our world has finally sunk its claws into her. Like they're taming her. I don't want that to happen.

"Grant Franklin Tavish the fifth," my mother says, every syllable like a tiny assault. "You missed your portrait sitting. *Again*. Look at this." She leads me into the formal living room, yanking the sheet off an easel, revealing the half-finished painting. The body is done, my hair looks okay, but my face is a blurry mass of flesh-colored paint. It's disconcerting to look at, but there's something about it that feels exactly right. This is probably the closest likeness they'll ever capture, and they don't even know it.

"I've rescheduled for Tuesday," she says as she covers it back up. "Please don't mar your face in any way on that trip. Not a scratch . . . do you understand me?"

"I'll do my best."

She takes a closer look at me, unsure if I'm being co-operative or mocking her. "Why are you so sweaty?"

I start to open my mouth to spill out some lame excuse, when she holds her hand up.

"Wait. Don't tell me." She closes her eyes and takes a

deep breath. "Marvin said you were meeting a *friend*. I'm glad you're getting out and about again, but please use protection. That's all we need."

I feel the heat take over my face.

"Gross," my sister hisses at me as she pushes me into the dining room.

"There you are," my dad says, making a big show out of our arrival. "I was beginning to wonder if I'd be dining alone."

"Wishful thinking," Mare murmurs, before crossing over to give him a hug.

I have to give my dad credit. He's a devoted family man. He could stay in DC, but he makes it home almost every night in time for dinner.

"Is that your latest?" my sister asks, pointing to the carved duck on the mantle.

"A teal. Isn't he a beauty?"

My dad is obsessed with ducks. Not feeding them at a pond, not studying their migration patterns, not even really shooting them. He's all about the decoy. He carves them himself. Hand paints them. The art of illusion, which I find ironic.

My mother moves stealthily behind him, straightening one of her ridiculously expensive porcelain bunny figurines that he accidentally knocked askew. For every new duck, Mom gets a new bunny. The silent duck-bunny war has been raging on for years.

Sometimes, when we're eating dinner, I see him staring off at his ducks, while she looks at her bunnies, and I wonder what they're thinking about. What their love for these inanimate objects says about them. Says about us.

As our maid, Mrs. Leaver, sets the table, we take our seats.

My father asks us all the right questions: How was your game? How did debate team go? Are you working on a new science project? Occasionally, he'll even make his eyes sparkle, the way he does for the cameras.

A few years ago, after dinner, I saw the card in the trash. Talking points my mother had given him so he can appear involved. Interested. As if he were speaking to some Rotary club, not having dinner with his family.

Tonight seems all the more painful. The awkward silences are punctuated by the ice in Dad's Scotch rattling along with my mother's jeweled bracelets.

"So, you're really doing it?" my father finally asks.

"Yes, sir." I sit up straight and clear my throat. "I'm taking the same route as you did, dropping in the second entrance at Crystal Falls. It's a two-mile hike to Widow's Peak, and from there I'll make the ascent at Custer's Chimney."

"One look at Widow's Peak and you might change your mind." He smiles. "But you can always backtrack, use the kiddie entrance. No shame in that."

"I won't change my mind," I assure him as I force another forkful of chicken into my mouth. It's clear he doesn't think I have what it takes to do this.

"Good . . . good." He nods in approval. "You better eat up, because that's the last protein you're going to have.

Unless of course you change your mind about hunting." He rests his knife on his plate, giving me a smug smile. "Hunger will do that to a man."

"A few days of nuts and berries won't kill him," my sister says.

My mother takes a healthy sip of her wine. "I still don't understand why he can't take a few granola bars . . . a bottle of water. In case of emergency."

"That's not how I did it. How my dad did it, and his dad before him." He sets down his glass a little too hard. "You live off the land. This is a sacred Tavish tradition."

Looking up at the line of portraits, of Tavish men, I can't help feeling like one of those decoys. A lesser copy of my dad. And maybe he feels the same way about his dad. We weren't great because of the things we did. We were great because of what our ancestors accomplished . . . and at what cost? Building an empire on the backs of the less fortunate. We carry on these traditions not out of respect or duty but out of fear. The fear of failure. Not measuring up.

Mom clears her throat and my father looks over on cue. She dabs at the corner of her mouth and he does the same. They have their own language like that. I'm not even sure if he had something on his mouth. Maybe she just wanted to remind him of her presence. How much he needs her.

Mare kicks me under the table, quickly opening her mouth to show me her chewed up food. I press my lips together to stifle a smile. I guess we have a language too, the kind that leaves bruises.

"I'm envious," my father says, his eyes misting over. "You're on the cusp of adulthood, your whole life ahead of you. A new beginning. Mark my words, this trip will make a man out of you."

Mare rolls her eyes. "It's four days, caving and camping in a tourist trap."

My dad ignores her, squinting his eyes like he does before he's about to make an important point in a speech. "You're going to feel real hunger. Real fear. Real appreciation and contentment for the first time in your life. You might not ever want to come back."

And there's something about that statement that gets to me. My dad talks about the trail like it was the best time in his entire life. Four days, alone in wilderness. How sad is that?

As soon as my mom lowers her sorbet spoon for the final time, my dad says, "Well, that was a lovely dinner. Give my compliments to Gladys. The roast chicken was excellent tonight."

I'm expecting him to head down to his workshop, but instead he pauses behind me, placing his hand on my shoulder. It feels heavy. Like my bones might collapse under the weight of what he's about to say. "Grant, I have something I want to show you."

Mare gives me a knowing smile as she excuses herself to go upstairs.

"Don't stay up too late, you two." Mom air kisses us both on the cheek. "Little Grant has a big day tomorrow."

As my mother heads to her bedroom, where she'll take

an Ambien and doze off listening to motivational speeches, I follow my dad outside.

The air is colder than I expected, but spring can be unpredictable like that. I wonder how cold it will be in the cave. How long I'll last down there.

As we stroll down the covered porch, past the columns, the rosebushes, I see exactly what this is all about. Just the sight of it floods the back of my throat with acid, but I choke it back down.

There, sitting in the drive, is a brand-new Range Rover with a red bow on top. It's not even a car, really. It's a tank.

I rock back on my heels, feeling like I'm going to pass out, but I force myself to stand up straight.

"We got silver this time," he says as he hands me the keys.

I try to hand them back. "I still can't–"

"As of four twenty-four P.M. this afternoon, your license has officially been restored."

"But I thought–"

"Monday's just a formality." He swipes a cottonwood seed off the hood. "You do what the lawyers tell you to do and all this will go away. You've got graduation, a summer abroad, maybe meet a few French girls, and then college. Everything will be back to normal before you know it."

Normal? I want to scream.

After what I did, should any of this be normal?

But I smile instead. Because that's what he wants. That's

what everyone expects of me. To feel grateful for all of this.

"Want to take it for a spin?" he asks.

The idea of getting behind the wheel again makes me feel sick to my stomach.

"I wish," I manage to get out. "But I've got to work on my paper . . . Lord Byron."

"You're still into poetry, huh?"

"Yeah, I guess so." I look down the drive, past the gate, anywhere but here.

I get the implication. Real men, *Tavish* men, aren't into poetry.

"I want you to know that I understand." He looks me straight in the eyes, which is something he hasn't been able to do since the incident. "We all have regrets. Things that bring us shame. In my day, it wasn't a crime unless you got caught. And with the media . . . it's a different world out there now." He puts his hands in his pockets. It makes me wonder what he got away with. "We all have to make tough choices in life, but it's how we deal with it that matters. That Tavish determination will see you through."

"I couldn't agree more," I reply.

I think about hugging him but, as if he can sense the incoming awkwardness, he reaches out to shake my hand.

Maybe I'm reading into things, but it feels like he understands *everything*. More than he cares to admit.

7

WHILE my dad escapes to the basement to drink Scotch and whittle his ducks, I walk through the house, taking it all in. The smell of oiled soap on wood floors, polished silver, thick, soft rugs dampening the sound of my heavy footsteps. Old photographs and antique letter openers adorning the tables. Chandeliers and chinoiserie wallpaper. People say the house you grow up in is a map to your childhood. But all I see is perfection. I don't see the spot where I spilled cranberry juice on the rug. I don't see the dent in the banister where I ran into it with my tricycle. I don't see the ink marks by the back hallway closet where my sister and I measured each other to see who was taller.

The rug had been replaced. The banister repaired. The plaster repainted.

But it went well beyond that.

Going up the first flight of stairs, I smooth my hand over the wall on the second floor, where the nursery used to be. He was only with us for six weeks. He died of SIDS—sudden infant death syndrome. There was no funeral. No one spoke his name. They plastered right over the door, as if they could erase him from existence. I wonder if that's what will happen to me.

As I'm heading up to the third floor, I see the light on in my sister's room. I can't remember the last time I went in there. I push the door open a crack. She's on the computer, doing homework, music blaring. Her hair's pulled back in a messy bun, and there's little dots of white cream on her face.

I knock and she flinches.

"You scared the crap out of me. I almost swallowed my retainer," she says as she twists around in her chair and throws a pillow at me. "So . . . new car, huh?"

"Yeah," I say, looking around at all the ticket stubs and photographs pinned to her corkboard.

"Are you nervous?" she asks.

"Not really." I put my hands in my pockets so I don't give myself away. "I've been planning for months. So what if I starve for a couple of days?"

"No . . . I mean about the other thing . . . on Monday." Even Mare can't say it out loud, and she's fearless. "You don't have to do anything you don't want to."

"Same goes for you," I say as I pull down the boarding school brochure from under a pile of to-do lists and other meaningless junk.

"Please," she says as she glances at it. "Like they're ever going to let me go."

"Maybe they'll surprise you. You should at least apply . . . see what happens." I set the brochure in front of her. "If you set your mind to something, you can do anything."

"So can you."

I lean over and hug her, which is probably overkill, but I think I'll regret it if I don't. "See you, weirdo."

"See you, loser."

I walk down the long hall, making a point not to look at the photographs lining the walls, but I can feel my younger self staring back at me. Judging me.

As soon as I close my bedroom door behind me, I let out a ragged breath—every bit of rancid air I've been holding inside. I'm looking around for something to do, busywork, but my room is beyond clean. I've always been tidy, but the past few months I've gotten worse. Outside of this room, I try to keep it in check, but this is the one place I can let my neat freak flag fly.

But I finally have actual things to attend to. Important things.

I was smart enough not to write anything down, but I've been making this checklist for months. I have it memorized.

And now the time has finally come.

Turning on my computer, I pull up my Byron paper. A little over three-quarters of the way done, which is perfect.

I read over it one last time and decide to take out a quote.

> *I had a dream, which was not all a dream.*
> *The bright sun was extinguish'd, and the stars*
> *Did wander darkling in the eternal space,*
> *Rayless, and pathless, and the icy earth*
> *Swung blind and blackening in the moonless air . . .*

It's my favorite, but it might be a little too heavy-handed. The last thing I want to do is raise any red flags.

Grabbing the housing preference sheet for GW off my corkboard, I fill it out.

I have no preferences. That was easy.

Next up, I sly dial Mary Grace Wells. As planned, it goes straight to voicemail. "Hey, Mary Grace, it's Grant. I'm getting ready to head out for my trail trip for a couple of days, but I was wondering, when I get back, if you might want to hang out. Grab dinner or something. Okay, well, have a great weekend."

My palms are sweaty. I'm out of practice. Of course, my mother would've been thrilled with that scenario. The Tavish and the Wells families go way back.

As I'm getting ready to shut down my computer, a chat window pops up in the right-hand corner.

Bennett101: *No way! You got your internet back. Finally.*

I write back. *Guess so.*

> Bennett101: *Sure you don't want to ditch the cave, come*
> *to the beach with us? I could pick you up at the trail,*
> *drop you back off on Sunday. They'd never know.*
> GTAV-V: *No. It's cool. I'm kind of looking forward to it.*
> *But thanks.*

Hey, Bennett—

I'm staring at the blinking cursor, thinking about everything we've been through together. Boy Scouts, summer camp, how we used to hide under the floating dock to avoid swim practice, studying for the SATs, trusting me with his secret and not getting mad when I didn't feel the same. There are a hundred things I want to type—*Thanks for being my friend. Thanks for trying to cheer me up. Thanks for never looking at me like I was some kind of monster.* But I don't.

I exit out. I'm about to shut it down when I decide to pull up Google search.

I'm staring at the box. I swallow hard at the prospect. All this time I've been wanting to face the truth, and now that I have it right at my fingertips, I'm scared to look.

I type in "Grant Tavish V" and hit Return.

Four people killed in tragic—

I exit out. Clean my browser and shut it down.

My heart's pounding so fast I think it might burst out of my rib cage.

I get up and pace the floor. Dragging my hands through

my hair, I try to remember to breathe. *You're almost there. Just stick to the plan.*

Grabbing my hiking pack out of the closet, I rush around the room, doing the rest of the things on my list. I wanted to take my time, put thought and purpose into every action, but now I just want to get it over with as quickly as possible. I need to keep reminding myself that tomorrow I'll be on the trail, making my descent at Crystal Falls, where all I have to think about is my next step, my next breath. Where everything is up to me.

I stand in front of my corkboard. The court summons stares back at me.

It's the one thing left hanging over me.

Taking down the flimsy sheet of paper, I open my desk drawer and bury it. Not at the bottom, like I was trying to hide from it. Not at the top, like it was foremost on my mind. But somewhere in the middle. Like it was just another thing I had to take care of.

8

"YOU don't remember anything."

I shoot up in bed, dripping with sweat, chest heaving. My eyes dart around the room, landing on everything that's familiar—everything that will never be the same.

But as soon as I put my feet firmly on the ground, I remember what today is. What it means.

I get dressed, brush my teeth, and force myself to leave a crumpled pair of pajama pants on the floor.

As I head downstairs, I pause on the second-floor landing.

There's a woman in a long, pale pink robe, standing next to the wall where the nursery used to be. At first I think it's a ghost, a figment of my imagination. But when I step closer, I realize it's my mother. She looks tired. Older. Almost fragile.

"Is everything okay?" I ask.

She looks up, startled, tucking an envelope into her pocket. "Bad dreams. That's all." Her eyes veer toward the hidden door. It's the closest I've seen to an acknowledgment. I always thought she buried it because she didn't want to face it. But maybe no one let her face it. Maybe we had that much in common.

"I'm sorry if I woke you," I say.

"No. I was just coming up to check on you."

Thinking I must've slipped up somehow, a wave of panic rushes through me. "Why?"

"Just to say . . . good luck," she says as she steps behind me, messing with my pack. "Are you sure this isn't too heavy?" She tugs on the straps.

"It's fine. I'm used to taking a lot more gear with me when I go on a day hike."

"Your keys are on the entry table."

"I've got an Uber meeting me at the gate. I figured it's probably not a good idea to ditch a brand-new car out there. Besides, I have no idea where I'll come out."

"Marvin can pick you up. Or *I* can pick you up."

I'm surprised by her offer to drive me herself, but I don't have time for this. "No. This is good. And I'll be seriously ripe after four days of–"

"You don't have to do this," she says quietly. "You don't have anything to prove."

I swallow hard, trying to keep my tone as even as possible. "But I do."

She takes my hand and squeezes it, the same way I did with her in the car yesterday. It's all I can do to hold it together.

"See you," I say as I pull away from her and head down another flight of stairs, out the front door, into the crisp morning air. I don't dare look back. I can't bear to see my mother's haunted face staring after me through the windows.

Maybe it's my imagination, but it felt like she was saying good-bye.

Being mindful of the cameras lining the drive, watching my every move, I look straight ahead.

I can just hear them now: *Did he look tired? Did he look confused? Did he look sad? Did he seem overconfident?*

I exit the gate and get into the back of the waiting car. The driver doesn't need to say a word. I can tell by the way he's looking at me that he knows exactly who I am.

Grant Franklin Tavish V.

A murderer.

9

AN hour and twenty-nine minutes later, we arrive at the Crystal Falls parking lot. It's jammed with school buses. There's a WELCOME RICHMOND PUBLIC SCHOOLS OUTDOOR CLUB banner hanging between two trees.

"No," I whisper as I get out of the car, slinging my pack over my shoulders.

I should've checked to see if there were any events out here today. And that makes me wonder how many other things I missed. It might be that one tiny overlooked detail that unravels my whole story. Unclenching my fists, I take a deep breath. Instead of obsessing, beating myself up over it, I keep my head down, trying my best to blend into the scenery. But as I make my way to the main trail, it's pretty clear I don't belong with this group. These are city kids.

People are running around, screaming and laughing. There's a group of girls freaking out because they saw a spider.

It's annoying, for sure, but that's not what really gets to me. They're all bursting with life. Promise. I don't even remember what that feels like. I almost don't want to get too close . . . afraid it will rub off on me.

As I pass by the main entrance to the caves, I see most of them are crowded around the first pitch. The chaperones are trying to get them lined up to take a turn on the harness so they can practice dropping in. It's only about a fifteen-foot drop, but from the way everyone's reacting, you'd think they were jumping off the James River Bridge.

Everyone's hollering and acting out, like they've never been in the woods before. Except for one girl, standing perfectly still as a flurry of movement surrounds her. She almost looks like a statue. Tall, athletic build, track pants and a sweatshirt, but she looks regal in a way. When she glances back at me, I get the strangest sensation, like I've seen her before. I shouldn't have made eye contact. I need to keep a low profile. I can't let anything get in my way at this point. Hopefully she didn't recognize me.

"Just stay focused," I say to myself as I hurry past them, making my way farther up the trail to the second entrance, the one reserved for more experienced cavers. But as I clear a cluster of pines, I see it's been taped off. A sheet of paper pinned to it. TEMPORARILY CLOSED.

"You've got to be kidding me." I let my pack fall off my shoulders, and look at my watch. I haven't even started and I'm already off schedule. I start pacing around the drop point.

"Okay, think." I snatch a leaf off one of the trees and start picking it apart.

I guess I could hike ahead to Custer's Chimney, drop in there, and then backtrack, but that's four miles from here. Logically, I wouldn't do that. If I hit a snag like this, I'd just skip the cave part of the trip and stay on the trail . . . but I can't do that. Too much has gone into this.

A couple of people scream and laugh from the school group. I peer back through the foliage. I've memorized every square inch of this cave system from the guidebook, and both entrances intersect about a mile before Widow's Peak. It would only add an hour or so to my schedule, but there must be a hundred kids crowded around the entrance, waiting for their turn. It's going to take forever to get through all of them, and if I go over there, asking if I can cut ahead, everyone's going to notice me. And then they'll tell the press what an impatient jerk I was. I can't have that.

No. I either have to wait or . . .

A gust of air bellows up from the taped-off entrance, making the sign flutter.

Looking around, I make sure no one's watching and then slip under the tape to stare down into the crevice.

Why not? It's not like it's blocked off with anything serious . . . just a flimsy strand of construction tape. Maybe they just did this because of the school trip. A liability thing.

And the fact is, if I don't do this now, I may never find the nerve again.

Putting on the extra layers, a pair of Gore-Tex pants and an all-weather coat, I secure my harness and head-lamp and toss my pack down to the ledge below. Now I have no choice but to go in after it. Slipping my rope through the anchor that's already embedded in the rock wall, I give it a hard tug, just to make sure it's secure, before I attach it to the harness. It's only about a forty-foot drop; I could easily free-climb it. But I need to get used to the harness, figure out the weak spots, before I reach the big drop at Widow's Peak.

As I look over the edge again, an ill wind seems to rush up from below, brushing my hair back from my face—almost like it's trying to tell me something. I know this cave is just a piece of limestone buried beneath the surface, but as I stare into the void, my headlamp illuminating the unknown, I can't shake the feeling that it's strangely alive, like I'm dropping into the mouth of some ancient monster. Maybe that's only fitting.

The truth is that, while I changed, the world stood perfectly still. Everyone said it would fade over time, but it felt like this festering sore. Every day the bacteria multiplied until the heat of infection spread from my belly to my heart. It was fatal.

Letting out a shaky breath, I think about the months of planning and preparation it took to get here. I made sure everyone knew I was looking forward to the trip. Bennett, Parker, and even Catherine will be interviewed, saying I was in good spirits. People saw me running from class, excited for break. I was seen at Outdoor World buying all the right equipment. I had a little bit of trouble when I forgot the ascent gear, but I think that might actually work in my favor. He'll tell the police I seemed a little too eager. I ate my dinner, even took seconds to show I had a hearty appetite. My paper was nearly done, clear of any quotes that could possibly be misconstrued. I filled out my housing questionnaire for GW. I even called a girl, asking her out on a date. Bennett and I have a tee time for next Friday. I left a pair of pajama pants on my bathroom floor. Neat, but not psycho neat. For all intents and purposes, I was a young man—full of promise, full of hope—whose life was cut short by a tragic accident. Nothing more. Nothing less.

My father will have the adventurous son he always wanted. My sister can use this tragedy to get to that boarding school, and my mom won't have to be reminded of her failure every time she looks at me. I'll just be another hidden door in the wall.

Yeah, I feel bad for doing this to my family, but I feel even worse for the families of my victims. I hope they can feel like they got some kind of justice. An eye for an eye.

I've been through every possible scenario a hundred times over, and this is the only way I don't have to betray my family, or betray myself. It's win-win. No one gets in trouble, no one gets hurt—well, except me. But accidents happen. And I made sure that's exactly what this will look like. That's life. I know firsthand how quickly everything can be taken away from you.

All I wanted to do was face the consequences of my actions.

But no one would let me.

Glancing up at the cloudless sky—a cross between Carolina blue and robin's egg—I take in one last hit of ozone.

I don't have any profound last words. There's no eleventh-hour reprieve.

"I'm sorry," is all I can manage to whisper before I take a giant leap backwards off the ledge, into nothing but air.

10

THE initial drop makes my stomach lurch in a way that's sickening and exhilarating all at once. As I brace my feet against the side of the rock wall for the first push back, a hint of a smile takes over my face. This is the first time in I don't even know how long that I feel fully in control. Down here, all I have to think about is my next move, my next breath. There's no one to judge me, no one to pity me. I'm not a senator's son or a murderer. And soon, I'll be free.

I'm about to push off again when I see a dark shadow looming overhead. I stop my descent, freezing in place. I'm bracing myself, waiting for someone to start yelling at me, telling me to get out of there, but all I hear is a whisper clinging to the stagnant air. The same wordless whisper that's plagued me since the incident.

What do they want from me?

By the time I work up the nerve to look up, they're gone.

I try to shake it off, because honestly, it doesn't matter anymore.

Whether it's some reporter looking for a story or a crazed vigilante wanting to scare me, they're too late. The next time they see me, I'll be in a mahogany box.

But as I'm preparing for my final leap to the chasm floor, I hear a strange set of popping noises, followed by a low grumble. I watch a deep crack traveling from the top of the drop all the way to the bottom, and before my brain can even process what's happening, the rock shelf below disintegrates, leaving nothing but dead space beneath me. I'm trying to scrabble up the rope when the rock slab I'm anchored to gives way.

I feel completely weightless as I plummet to the depths.

The walls are collapsing around me, kicking up ancient dust and debris, shards of limestone flying through the air with deadly force. I can't breathe, I can't see; I feel myself falling but I'm so disoriented I can't even tell if I'm falling down or falling up. It's like God has turned the world upside down, giving it a hard shake. This is what I wanted, but still I fight—against gravity, against nature, against my family, against myself—because in this moment, all I want to do is remember.

As I'm plunging through the darkness, I'm thinking

this is it, exactly what I deserve, when a chunk of rock breaks free from the slab I'm tethered to and comes hurtling toward me.

I feel a burst of warmth—

And then nothing.

11

I had a dream, which was not all a dream.
The bright sun was extinguish'd, and the stars
Did wander darkling in the eternal space,
Rayless, and pathless, and the icy earth
Swung blind and blackening in the moonless air . . .

I COME to, suspended in midair, dangling from my harness, like a fly caught in a web. Gasping for air, I cough up rocks and blood from my lungs. I can't feel my lower body, but when I shift my weight, tiny pinpricks of electricity flood my legs.

Looking up, I see the giant slab that I'm anchored into is wedged into the crevice. Nothing but an avalanche of boulders built up behind it, blocking out any light from the surface.

Letting out a shuddering breath, I force myself to look down. There's nothing but black. I pull out a shard of rock lodged in my harness and let it drop.

"One, one thousand," I count. "Two, one thousand. Three, one thousand. Four one thousand."

I swallow hard before continuing.

"Five, one thousand. Six, one thousand. Seven, one thousand."

I'm getting short of breath.

"Eight, one thousand. Nine, one thous–"

When the stone finally hits the bottom with a faint snap, tears sting the corners of my eyes, but I don't dare take my hands off the rope to wipe them away.

The bottom has dropped out, making this chasm deeper than Widow's Peak–deeper than my worst nightmare. It feels like a portal straight to hell.

And yet, for the violence that just occurred, it's eerily quiet. Like any hope of the outside world has been blotted out along with the sun. The only sounds I hear are a sporadic drip, rope scraping against the metal clamp, an occasional breeze wheezing through the cracks in the rock. Or maybe it's a whisper. Even down here I can't escape the feeling like there's someone with me. Watching. It's that same feeling you get when you rush down a dark stairwell, like something's right over your shoulder . . . breathing down your neck.

"Hello?" I whisper. And when I hear the distorted echo

whispered back to me, it makes me want to crawl out of my skin. All I can do is hang here like bait.

Starting to panic, I search my surroundings. I'm too far from the rock ledge on either side to even think about getting out of this, but there's a hazy beam of light streaming in from everywhere I turn.

"Is someone there?" I manage to choke out as I whip my head around, frantically trying to see where the light's coming from. My head's throbbing. Reaching up, I discover the source of the light—my headlamp—but I also find the left side of my hair is matted with dried blood. How long have I been hanging here? Hours . . . days? I look at my watch, but it's not working—stopped at 11:57 P.M.

If I dropped in around nine this morning, that means I've been hanging here for nearly fifteen hours. Maybe more.

As I stare down into the abyss, I remember why I came down here in the first place. I couldn't ask for a better scenario. It's like the universe is saying, *Let me help you with that.* No equipment failure, no human error . . . it's just a collapse. A natural death. All I have to do is detach from the rope and this will all be over.

In my head, this seemed like the easiest decision I'd ever have to make, but now, faced with the nothingness, the cold, the deep, I can't help but wonder if I'm making a huge mistake.

But it's too late for any of that now.

As I slide my hand down the rope and place it on top

of the carabiner, the rock above me grinds down a few inches, making my heart stutter.

"Wai . . . wai . . . wait," I say through gritted teeth as I grip on even tighter.

Pressing my forehead against the rope, I start to cry. Something I haven't done since the night of the incident. I'm not even sure who I'm crying for. The truth is, I'm angry. Angry at the hand I've been dealt, at my family for not letting me face the consequences, at myself for not having the balls to face them. I always thought I was a decent guy. Why did it have to be me on that road, on that night, at that exact moment? What was the point of all this?

But when I think of the *real* victims, all the pain I've caused, I know what I have to do. I don't deserve to walk away from this unscathed.

The way I see it, I have two choices. I can either hang here, starve to death, wait for the inevitable further collapse. Or I can take matters into my own hands and finish what I started.

With tears streaming down my face, I reach up to unscrew the safety latch on the carabiner, but it's jammed. Either it's frozen shut or my hands are too cold and swollen to function properly. "Please," I say as try to get it to move, but it won't budge.

"Help me," I cry in frustration, and the rock grinds down another inch.

As I hang there, limp and exhausted, I start to laugh

at the absurdity of it all. How, even now, at the end of it all, I still can't get anything to go my way.

"If that's how you want it . . . just do it!" I scream, opening my hands wide, but nothing happens.

I start searching my pockets for anything I can use to help me open the latch, when I find the Swiss Army knife. Digging it out, I run my thumb over the monogram. GFT V. My dad gave this to me when I turned ten. I remember how excited I was to get one just like his. I almost feel guilty using it for this, but Dad said this trip would make a man out of me.

As I open the blade, my chin begins to quiver.

"Forgive me," I whisper as I press the blade against the rope.

"Hey," a faint voice echoes through the cavern.

Holding still, I glance over my right shoulder and see a headlight swerving up ahead.

For a moment, I wonder if I did it, if I'm already dead, caught in a nightmare, an endless loop of that night . . . but as the glow gets closer, I realize it's a flashlight.

The light skims across my face. I fold the blade, concealing it in the palm of my hand.

A rescue team. Damn.

But I can still do this. All I have to do is stall them. This entire system is on the verge of collapse, and if worse comes to worst I can always distract them and slice the rope when they're not looking.

"I'm here," I reply, shielding my eyes.

"Thank God," someone says.

As they emerge from a tunnel on my right, I see their silhouettes. The biggest one steps forward to peer over the drop and then quickly backs away, clinging to the inside of the tunnel. "You have no idea how happy we are to see you."

"Is it just you?" another one calls out.

I shift my weight. "Yeah, I think so."

"But we heard you talking to some—"

"It's just me," I cut them off.

"How should we do this?" a female voice says. "Are you going to take us one at a time?"

"Wait . . ." I call back. "Aren't you the rescue team?"

"Hardly," a skinny guy says with a strangled laugh. "We thought *you* were."

"No," I call back, relief and dread consuming me at once.

"So we're stuck down here . . . same as him?" the bigger guy says, a nervous edge to his voice.

"Well, not as stuck as *him*," the skinny guy replies. "That would really suck."

"Shut up. You're freaking him out," a second, shorter girl says as she slaps him in the chest.

The school group. It must've been their turn in the pitch when the collapse happened.

A horrible realization comes over me. Did I do this? Am I the reason they're trapped down here?

The cave lets out a grumble of warning.

"You have to get out of here," I say.

"You need to figure out how to get over to us." The first girl shines her light over the scene.

"We don't have time for that, and I can't do anything without my pack—"

"You mean this?" She shines her light on my backpack, the strap clinging to a jagged rock.

"Look," I say as I squeeze the blade in my hand. "Even if we could figure something out, it's too unstable. Any extra pressure on this thing and the whole system's going to collapse. You should take my pack, find a way out—"

"Find a way out?" The skinny kid pulls the pack off the rock. "Don't you think we tried that?"

"For real." The smaller girl shivers. "I feel like we've been down here forever . . . walking in circles."

"You need to go east, toward the main entrance." I grunt in pain as I shift my weight again. "Just follow the water patterns in the rock. They're bound to lead you to an exit."

"Do we look like we know anything about water patterns?" he says as he rifles through my bag. "We don't even know how to use any of this stuff."

"But *he* does," the tall girl says, shining her light on me.

A tremendous groan echoes through the cavern as the rock slab grinds down a few more inches, peppering me with limestone.

"Just get to the surface and you can send for help. I'll be—"

"We're not leaving you." The tall girl zeros in on me. "Either you figure out how to reach us, or we'll start improvising."

I don't know what my face is doing, but I'm completely terrified. This is the last thing I need right now.

When I don't reply, she grabs one of the ropes out of my pack. "Fine." Nodding toward a jagged pinnacle formation on the right, she says, "Somebody kick that rock."

"Why?" the shorter girl asks.

"We need to see how secure it is. If it will hold his weight."

"Are you sure that's a—"

The ceiling grinds down another inch, making all the hair on my arms stand on end. "Please, just go. You don't want to be anywhere near this place when it—"

"Darryl . . . do it," the main girl says, completely ignoring me.

"Look, I know I'm fat but—"

"Stop," the smaller girl says as she reaches out to rub his arm. "She's not saying that. It's just because you took jujitsu."

"That was *one* time at the park, because it was free. I should've never told you guys about that."

"Come on," the tall girl yells.

He gives it a solid kick—it doesn't budge.

"Okay, loop the rope around and toss him the end."

"You should throw it, Shy," the skinny guy says.

"Shy?" I ask, feeling more frustrated with every passing second.

"Short for Shyanne. Discus. All state." He shoves the rope into the taller girl's hands. "She's going to the Olympics."

"He doesn't need my life story," the girl mutters. "I can get the rope to you, but you better be ready for it."

Before I can get a word out, she twists her torso, winds her arm back and then whips it across the cavern. It catches me right across the back, before falling to the depths.

"Oof. That's going to leave a mark," the skinny one says.

As she hauls it back up, I hear a few of them whispering, probably wondering if this is a lost cause, but the girl stays focused, staring at me unflinchingly. I don't know if she's doing this to try to encourage me, but it's beyond intimidating. "You're going to have to do better than that," she says.

"I'm sorry." I let out a ragged breath as I shift my weight again. "But you're wasting your time. This isn't going to work."

She steps all the way to the edge. I think she's going to yell at me, but she softens her tone. "I know you're probably tired. We're all tired. But you're going to have to dig deep. We have to do this together."

The slab of limestone grinds down another inch, making me shudder.

Closing my eyes, I take a few deep breaths. Clearly, there's no way this girl is going to give up, and if this collapses while they're trying to help me, they'll be buried right along with me. The last thing I want right now is to be rescued, but I can't have any more blood on my hands. I just can't.

"Ready," I call out as I readjust in the harness and propel my body around.

She hurls the rope in my direction and I lurch forward, barely snatching it out of the air.

They all cheer, which makes the entire chasm tremble.

"Shh . . ." someone whispers.

"Loop it through the clamp on your vest thingy and tie it off," she says as she proceeds to get everyone lined up on the other end of the rope, taking the front position. "Now all you have to do is free yourself from the old rope."

"Are you crazy?" the bigger guy says in alarm. "He probably weighs a hundred and eighty pounds. We can't hold him. It's suicide."

Finally, a word of reason. I know they'll feel guilty leaving me, but that will quickly fade when they get out of here and find out who I was.

They're arguing over what to do when I say, "It doesn't matter anyway. Like I was trying to tell you, it won't work. The first rope . . . the carabiner is stuck. It won't budge."

Shy lowers her voice. "Then I guess you'll have to use the knife in your hand to cut it."

Gripping the Swiss Army knife, I can feel her dark eyes digging into me, like she knows everything.

"We can do this," Shy assures everyone.

I can tell they're scared, but they all seem to agree.

"We're counting on you," she says, turning her attention back to me, and I know exactly what she means. *Don't screw this up.*

It's so dark I can barely make out the details of her face, but I can feel her resolve. And if something goes wrong, I'm not sure she'll let go of the rope. She'll be the first to go over the edge.

As I open the blade, I realize I could cut through all the ropes at the same time. They wouldn't know I did it on purpose. They'd just think I made a mistake. It's dark. I'm exhausted. Accidents happen all the time down here.

"Cutting now," I say as I press the blade against the rope. I hear the unmistakable sound of fraying fiber. Every caver's worst nightmare. But it's like music to my ears. Because no matter what happens, that sound is going to set me free.

12

WHEN the rope snaps, I hear screams echoing through the cavern as I go slamming into the side of the chasm wall. There are grunts of exertion, skidding feet, tiny bits of rock falling from above, but by some miracle, it holds.

"Are you there?" someone calls down.

I try to answer, but I've had the wind knocked out of me.

"Dude, can you hear us?"

"We don't even know his name."

"Please, don't be dead," someone whispers.

As a flashlight glares down on me, I look up, meeting their eyes for the first time—four sets of eyes, glistening in the dark.

I take in a rasping breath. "I'm good."

As they pull me up, I glance back to where I was hanging. The severed red rope dangles there like a warning: this is how close you came to death.

As I get near the ledge, arms reach out for me.

"Stay back," I say as I dig my fingers into the wet rock. If I fall, I don't want to bring them down with me.

As I'm pulling myself up the last few inches, I lose my grip and begin to keel backwards. The taller girl grabs onto the strap of my harness. I cling to her for dear life. I'm almost embarrassed by how much my body wants to live in this moment. How it yearns for solid ground. After everything I've done, I don't deserve this, the kindness of these people who are probably stuck down here because of me. But this is bigger than me and my pathetic life right now.

As they drag me back from the ledge to the safety of the tunnel, the rock slab I was anchored into finally gives way, filling the chasm with an avalanche of stone in a matter of seconds.

The skinny one fans away the settling cloud of dust. "Guess we won't be going that way."

Looking back at how close they came to being trapped under all that makes me sick. I lean my head between my legs, trying to get ahold of myself, but the world is spinning out of control. I throw up. Nothing but liquid and bile.

"He needs water," the shorter girl says.

The skinny guy grabs the water bottle from my pack. "It's empty."

"Well, look around," she says. "This place is dripping with water."

"Not that we'd want to drink," the bigger guy adds. "Remember that little virus, Ebola? Found in a cave."

"Not now," the shorter girl says.

The main girl grabs the water bottle, fills it up with the water trickling down the side of the cave wall, and forces me to drink. It tastes of earth and metal; fine bits of grit coat my tongue, my teeth.

It's the first time I'm seeing her up close. She has long, dark curly hair that's been pulled back from her face. She looks vaguely familiar. "Shy, right?" I try not to stare too long. She's pretty, but there's a sharp edge about her. "I think I saw you when I hiked in for the drop. Do you remember me?"

"We don't need to be friends, okay? All we need you to do is get us out of here."

"Jesus, Shy. Ease up," the shorter one says. "He almost died."

"So did we. Saving his ass," she says as she takes the water away from me, wiping off the rim with the bottom of her sweatshirt.

I can't help but laugh at that. She actually thinks she did me a favor.

"Hey . . . don't worry about her." The other girl, the small one, crouches in front of me, shining her light on the side of my head. "That looks pretty nasty, but it's not bleeding anymore. Follow my finger with your eyes," she says as she checks my reflexes, my pulse. I don't think she likes what she feels, because she's scrambling to get me out of the harness.

I groan with how good it feels to be free of that thing. All I want to do is curl up on the floor and rest, but she won't let me.

"You can't close your eyes, not until I know you don't have a concussion," she says as she starts roughly squeezing my limbs.

"What are you doing?" the big guy asks.

"We need to get his blood circulating."

I study her face. She has on makeup . . . or she used to have on makeup. Most of it's melted off by now, but you can tell she's into that kind of thing. "How do you know about all this?"

"EMT training," she answers, blowing her bangs out of her eyes.

"Next step, med school," the big guy says as he stoops next to her to help out.

"Please. I'll be lucky if I can scrape enough money together for my phlebotomy certificate. What's your name?" she asks.

I glance over at Shy; she's whispering something to the skinny guy. No doubt something about me.

I think about lying, telling them it's Jack or John, but I'm sick of lying to everyone—lying to myself—and they deserve to know what kind of person they're down here with.

"Grant Franklin Tavish . . . the fifth."

Shy rolls her eyes. "First name would've sufficed."

I look around, and they're just staring at me blankly. *They don't know. They don't know who I am.*

"Shyanne Rose Taylor . . . the original," the tall girl says as she leans against the cave wall.

"But everyone calls her Shy," the other girl says, almost apologetically, as she finally stops pounding on my legs. "I'm Maria. Maria Priscilla Perez."

"Priscilla?" the lanky guy laughs.

"What?" Maria stands up, dusting off her skinny jeans. "My mommy's an Elvis fan."

"Darryl James Arnold," the bigger guy says. He wraps his arms around Maria to warm her up, but I know he's also doing it to send me a message: hands off.

The other guy steps forward with a wide, easy grin. "I'm Kit." He reaches out to shake my hand; it's colder than mine. "Real name is Jeremiah George Jackson. At least that's the name the state gave me."

"Where does Kit come from?" Darryl asks.

"Kit Kats," he says as he blows into his hands and then shoves them in the pocket of his hoodie. "Fourth grade, I found a rolled-up twenty outside that house on Hay Street."

Shy shakes her head. "You're lucky some tweaker didn't come out looking for it."

"Truth," he says with a booming laugh. "But instead of spending it on a bunch of junk, I bought one of those jumbo packs of Kit Kats. Made a sign about needing to raise money for soccer uniforms. For some reason, rich people love soccer."

"Normally, I'd argue with you about gross stereotypes like that," Darryl says as he scratches his fresh buzz cut, "but I think you might be right on that one."

"Took the bus to the mall and sold them for two bucks a pop. Quadrupled my money in a day," he says as he flips up his hood. "And an empire was born."

"Hustler from birth." Shy glares at him.

"Knock it all you want, but how do you think I got my Xbox?"

"It's still wrong."

"Well, I don't have a Grandma Ruth taking care of me."

"Then why is she always feeding you?"

"You know what I mean. I wasn't begging. I wasn't stealing. The way I look at it, for a couple of bucks people get to feel good about themselves, and they get a damn good candy bar on top of that. Win-win."

"You never got busted?" Darryl asks.

"Not really. Couple times 'concerned mothers' called mall security. But one time, down by the capitol, this guy in a nice suit gave me a hundred for my moxie. I had to look it up . . . it basically means 'balls.'"

I can't help wondering if it was my dad or one of his friends who did that. They probably went back to the office, talking about this kid . . . how he could have a bright future in politics. An amusing story for their next cocktail party. But they didn't do anything to really help him.

"What are you doing down here . . . by yourself?" Shy asks, eyeing the expensive watch on my wrist. "Pretty sure you don't belong with the Richmond Public Schools Outdoor Club."

I pull my sleeves down over my hands. "I go to St. Augustine."

"La-di-da," Kit says.

"It's a graduation trip." I try to stretch out my legs. "Kind of a rite of passage in my family. My dad did it, his dad before him. Becoming a man and all that." I didn't mean to give that much info, but I'd rehearsed that answer so much it just kind of spilled out of me.

"Then why don't you have any food or water in your pack?" Shy grills me.

"It's a survival trip." I meet her gaze. "That's kind of the whole point."

"So, your dad's a real hard-ass." Darryl perks up. "Military?"

"Something like that," I murmur.

Shy stares at me. That same look she gave me when I passed her on my way to the drop point, like she can see right through me.

I tear my eyes away from her. "What happened to you guys?"

"We don't know," Kit says. "One minute we were fine, joking around, laughing, and then *boom*."

Maria's eyes veer toward the dark passageway. "We kept following the tunnel, and then we heard you yelling."

"How long have we been down here?" I ask as I lean my throbbing head against the rock.

"We don't know that, either." Darryl sighs.

"What do you mean you don't know?"

"Look around . . . Could be three in the afternoon or three in the morning."

"It feels like we've been down here for months," Maria says, flinching at a drop of water that falls from the ceiling.

"Don't you have watches? Phones?"

"Check it out," Darryl says as he pulls his flip phone out of his pocket, and nods to the others to do the same. "They all stopped working at the same time—eleven fifty-seven P.M."

"Mine too." I rub my thumb over my watch.

Darryl leans in, nudging my knee. "I've been thinking. Maybe there's some weird frequency down here. Electrons in the rocks. Or some military device. They have those now. Things that can scramble your electronics."

"Why would anyone do that?" Maria sighs.

"To cut off communication. Think about it. This would be the perfect cover for a secret military facility. For all we know, there could be a secret door or hatch around here somewhere."

"Spare us the conspiracy theories," Shy says.

"I'm serious. They have secret labs hidden all over the place. Why not here?"

Kit shines his flashlight around the dull, confined space. "What could they possibly be hiding in this hellhole?"

"Caves are the last frontier, right? The eighth continent, really. I read about these extremophiles . . . life forms they can't even identify. Who knows what's down here. On episode six of *Ancient Aliens* there's this—"

"You need to stop watching that garbage." Maria smacks his arm. "It's warping your mind." She turns to me. "Don't let him scare you."

"What if it's some kind of experiment?" Darryl lifts his brows. "A government thing."

"Or someone looking for revenge." I glance back toward the collapsed entry, wondering if the person who's been following me could've done this. Maybe they thought they were doing the world a favor, which wouldn't be wrong . . . but now there are innocent people involved. "Do you think they sell scramblers like that online?" I ask.

"I know they do," Darryl replies, without the slightest hesitation.

"Please tell me you're not buying into all of this," Maria says. "It doesn't make any sense. Why would someone do that? Terrorize a bunch of people trapped in a cave?"

Kit bursts out laughing. "You just described at least a dozen horror movies. But no one we know could afford a piece of equipment like that, and I seriously doubt squeaky-clean-jeans over here has any enemies."

Shy looks at me, and I feel something twist inside of

me. Either she knows something or I'm just being paranoid. Either scenario isn't good.

"Wait," Kit whispers. "Do you hear that?"

"Now you're freaking *me* out." Maria rubs her arms.

I sit up, straining to hear it. Maybe he hears the whisper, too.

"It's the sound of Darryl's sanity, floating away in the wind," Kit says as he pretends to watch something drift down the tunnel.

"Very funny." Darryl crosses his arms over his chest.

"Yeah, well, I hate to interrupt your paranoia party," Shy says, "but since I don't see any military personnel coming to our aid, or some psycho coming to terrorize us, we need to get moving."

"Do you think you can stand?" Maria asks.

"Yeah," I answer, without even thinking, but as I try to get up, my legs fold beneath me.

"Hey, take it easy," Darryl says, gripping my elbow.

"I'm fine. I can walk. Just let me—"

"You heard him. Get him on his feet."

"Shy, no," Maria pleads. "Look at him."

"If he says he can walk, he can walk. If he needs help, he needs to ask for it."

"Believe me," I say as I struggle to get up on my own, "I want to get this over with as much as you do."

13

AS we form a single-file line to get through the tunnel, I take the last position. One, I don't want them staring at me, figuring out who I am; and two, I'm not even sure if I can do this.

The first few steps are the worst. It feels like my bones are made out of thin glass, but as my muscles slowly start to warm back up, it gets a little easier.

The good thing is we have to take it slow. Even with my headlamp and all the flashlights on, it's dark. The kind of dark that pushes back against you, like it doesn't want to be illuminated.

The ground's fairly even so far, but there are stagnant

pools of water everywhere. And I'm pretty sure I'm the only one wearing the right gear. Shy has on a decent pair of running shoes, Maria, a pair of ankle boots, clearly made for fashion, not function. Kit has on a pair of worn-out Converse and Darryl's wearing the soggiest Timberlands I've ever seen. They must weigh a ton.

The cave walls aren't smooth like I expected; they're rough, with jagged spikes sticking out from every direction, just waiting for the opportunity to draw blood.

It feels unnatural, like we're not supposed to be down here. Even the air feels foreign, like it's too thick for my lungs.

A strange breeze brushes past my cheek, like someone's behind me, whispering in my ear. I stop and turn. Beyond the ghastly shadows from my headlamp, the soft music of the water seeping through the stone, there's nothing there. At least nothing I can see.

"You better keep up, Chad," Shy calls back.

"It's Grant," I say with a deep sigh, as I continue forward.

"Whatever."

As I listen to them talking about everything from their teachers to basketball to the last thing they ate, my irritation grows. I shouldn't even be here right now. I don't belong with these people. And if rescue workers reach us before I can get them to the surface, all of this planning will be for nothing. I think about how easy it would be to take off my headlamp, set down my pack, and slip into one of the gnarled recesses. But, with my luck, they'd probably just end up wasting all their resources trying to find me. No. I need to at least get them on the right path, and then the rest is up to me. I can still pull this off.

As they begin to emerge from the twisted tunnel into some kind of cavern, Darryl says, "Whoa." I can tell the space is big by the way it echoes around the chamber.

I step through to find a towering room filled with boulders. The only way forward is at the top of the incline, a small craggy opening.

"At least it's going in the right direction," Maria says, staring up at the imposing obstacle.

"Maybe it's a way out," Darryl says.

"There's only one way to find out," Kit says as he charges ahead. As he leaps onto the first boulder, it teeters forward and the whole terrain begins to shift. He jumps off right before one of the rocks comes barreling down the incline. I feel the gust of air as it whooshes past me, exploding against the cave wall.

Kit laces his fingers behind his head, letting out a huge breath. "Man oh man, that was close."

"What is this place?" Maria says as she steps behind Darryl.

"It's a boulder choke," I say, staring up the incline. "This must've happened during the collapse. One wrong move and—"

"Splat." Darryl swallows hard enough that we hear it.

"How do we do this?" Shy asks.

"Maybe we can rig up one of Grant's ropes?" Kit shines his light on the ceiling. "Pull ourselves up."

"Like that scene from *Rambo* four, right?" Darryl goes to high-five him, but Kit just shakes his head.

"Do I look like I've seen *Rambo* four?"

"This is where *you* come in." Shy snaps her fingers in front of me. "What's our next move?"

"I'm thinking," I say, swatting her hand away. I'm trying to remember anything about a boulder choke, but all I can recall is "steer clear," which isn't going to help.

Her eyes widen. "You don't know, do you?"

"Just give me a second . . . some room to breathe." I wipe the cold sweat from my brow with my sleeve. "I remember something about this from my class."

"Your class?" Shy balks. "So you've actually never seen one before?"

"Yeah. That's how people *learn* things." I steal a glance at her and wish I hadn't. "I may not remember every detail, but–"

"Why?" she needles me. "If you knew you were coming down here by yourself, with no food, no water, why wouldn't you have paid attention to every single detail? You don't strike me as stupid. Unless you've got some kind of death wish."

I open my mouth to reply, but nothing comes out. I don't even know how to begin to answer that.

"I see guys like you at meets all the time." She shakes her head. "You've got all the right gear, elite coaches, special training, the best that money can buy, but it's all just for show. Isn't it?"

I pretend I don't hear her.

"That's what I thought." She steps away.

"What . . . so we're basically screwed?" Daryl starts pacing in front of the boulders. "I knew this was a bad idea. But you're Maria's best friend. *Sure, come with,*" he says in a mocking tone. "*It'll be a blast,* she said."

"So this is *my* fault?" Shy raises her voice. "Excuse me for wanting to include you in something other than sitting around in your underwear watching TV."

"Hey," Maria says. "You don't have to talk to him like that."

"*Let's get out of the city, breathe clean air,*" Darryl says as he waves his arms around. "*I can borrow my grandma's car. It'll be such a pretty drive.*"

"Just shut up, Darryl," Kit says. "Don't you ever get tired of listening to your stupid voice?"

"You should talk." Maria turns on Kit.

I can't stand listening to them argue, especially when I know this is all my fault.

"Look, I can help." I step directly into the fray. "At least I knew what this thing is called. I've studied this cave system. I know it by heart. There are six exits to this system, and with the collapse there could be a lot more now."

"Or a lot less," Shy says, turning her full attention back on me. "I saw you heading for that second entrance, and we all know it was closed off. But you went in anyways, didn't you?"

"Come on, Shy." Kit comes to my defense. "Lay off."

"Why? He's the reason we're down here."

"Were you following me?" I ask, wondering if she could be the person I've been seeing all this time.

"Even if he did cause the collapse, he didn't do it on purpose," Kit says.

"Are you so sure about that?"

"*Why* would he do that?" Kit places his hand on her shoulder.

She pulls away from him. "Because, look at him . . ." she says as she gets in my face. "Rules don't apply to people like him. You think you're above everything, don't you?" She grabs onto my coat. "You think you're better than us."

I don't fight her. I don't struggle to get free. Instead, I look her dead in the eyes. "Actually, I think I'm the lowest form of scum on the planet."

This seems to catch her off guard.

"What's gotten into you?" Maria says as she pulls Shy off me.

She staggers back, taking in deep huffs of air.

"Everyone needs to calm it down," Kit says. "At Mo's junkyard I climb stuff like this all the time. Stacked-up cars, electronics. We just have to find the safest route. I'm quick on my feet." He looks back at Shy. "I can do this."

Shy takes in a few more deep breaths before giving him a slight nod.

"Kit," I call out, tossing him a roll of reflective tape from my pack.

He snatches it out of the air. "What's this for?"

"To mark your path for the others."

"Sweet," he says as he tears off a bunch of pieces, putting them on his hand for easy access.

Running with it, Kit flips up his hoodie and then ducks between two boulders, hoisting himself up on the biggest one. He grins back at us. "See, no sweat." But when it starts to rock, he quickly leaps onto a different stone and tags it.

We're all watching him with bated breath as he crawls, worms, and contorts his wiry frame through the maze of boulders to find a safe path.

When he finally reaches the top of the slope, he's just a hazy silhouette. And I can picture him, clear as day, standing on top of the junk pile as a kid, victorious.

"You guys aren't going to believe this," he says, panning his flashlight over the scene on the other side.

"Do you see light?" Shy asks with a shallow breath.

"No, but it looks like Santa's Village . . . from the mall."

"Great." Maria presses her lips together and nods. "He's hallucinating now."

While Kit directs them from above, Darryl goes next, followed by Maria.

I want to take this moment to say something to Shy, to explain myself, but what can I possibly say?

She's right. We're not friends. I don't know these people. And they don't want to know me. The best thing I can do is keep my mouth shut until I get them to the surface. They'll find out who I really am, what I've done, soon enough.

Shy goes next, vaulting onto the first boulder with ease.

I wait until she's halfway up, just to give her some space. I'm copying every hand placement, every curve of her foot, when I hear something sharp clattering against the rocks.

"What was that?" Kit calls down, shining his flashlight over the rocks.

"I told you guys I heard something earlier," Darryl whispers.

"No. It's just my stupid flashlight," Shy grumbles. "It slipped between the rocks, but I think I can get it." She shoves her arm through the gap, straining to reach it, when something shifts. I feel it before I can even see it, like one of those wind-up jack-in-the-box toys on the verge of springing open.

I start scrambling up the incline, when the boulder next to her begins to rock forward. Swinging my pack around, I shove it in the gap before it completely pulverizes her arm. She's fighting to pull herself free, but she's pinned, the rock holding her like a vise.

I crouch beside her, completely out of breath. The look on her face—it's like looking at a ghost. "Are you okay?"

She nods, but I can tell she's scared.

The stone lets out an angry groan like it's hungry.

Darryl shines his light directly on us. "What's going on?"

"I'm coming down," Kit says.

"Don't," I yell back, shielding my eyes. "Stay where you are . . . and get that light off of us."

As I'm trying to find a safe foothold, Shy whispers, "My arm."

"It's going to be okay," I murmur, but it looks bad. If this settles by even another half an inch, it's going to destroy her humerus.

"You don't understand," she says between clenched teeth. "I *need* this arm." Her eyes are glassy with fear. I've seen that look before.

"Discus, right?" I need to keep her talking while I figure out a way to free her without causing an avalanche.

"It's all I have." She winces as the stone grinds down another quarter centimeter. "If I lose this arm, I lose scholarships, sponsorship, the Olympics . . . any hope of taking care of–I can't lose this arm, do you get me?"

"I do." I give her a reassuring nod. "And I'm going to help you, but you have to listen to me. Focus. I'm going to push the rock back, but I'll only be able to hold it for a second. As soon as you feel it give, I need you to grab the pack and get to the top as fast as you can."

"But if it rolls back on you–"

"I don't care about that." I look her straight in the eyes. "Right now, all I care about is you . . . your arm. Okay?"

She shakes her head. "I can't–"

"You won't owe me anything. After this, we're even."

I can't tell if it's sweat or tears running down her face, but she manages to nod.

Digging my heels into the crack of an enormous boulder, I lean my shoulder against the rock and push with my entire body. "Go," I grunt.

As she pulls herself free, grabs the pack, and scrambles to the top, I feel the entire ground move beneath me. Maybe it's just my body trembling with the strain, but I feel like the stone is talking to me, telling me to let go. And I hope this is it, that I've served my purpose, found a sliver of redemption in the end. Maybe it's just the shock talking but, in this moment, I feel almost serene about the whole thing. I let go and close my eyes, waiting to be taken—waiting—but nothing happens.

Hearing them scream my name, I open my eyes to find boulders collapsing all around me. I look up and Shy is urging me to run . . . to live. All I want to do is stand here, wait for a boulder to take me, but if I don't at least try, she's going to have to carry around the guilt of my death for the rest of her life. I know all too well what that can do to a person.

I'll have to find another way.

Dodging stone and debris, I claw my way up the crumbling incline. My muscles are burning with fatigue, but the adrenaline takes over.

The roar of the stone crashing to the bottom is deafening, and by the time I reach the top, the entire landscape has changed, exposing a new layer of deadly stone beneath. Nature's booby trap. I stare into the dark tunnel below. If there's someone else down here, I'll definitely hear them coming.

As soon as I catch my breath, I dig my spare flashlight out of my bag and hand it to Shy.

I'm expecting a thanks, maybe a look of gratitude, but

she gives away nothing. If anything, I wonder if this made her hate me even more. I don't think she liked being that vulnerable in front of me. I'd never tell anyone, but, in that brief moment, I think I caught a glimpse of who she really is. She's tough, but there's a softness underneath all that. And maybe we're the same in that way, desperately trying to cling to our armor.

It's probably just exhaustion or the cold getting under my skin, but for some reason I can't stop wondering what a smile would look like on her face.

14

THEY all take turns sliding down a huge slab of stone into an enormous cavern filled with breathtaking gobs of crystal and shimmering white calcite formations dripping down like icing.

"What'd I tell you," Kit says as he spins around. "Welcome to Santa's Village."

"It's cold enough," Maria says with an audible shiver.

I slide down after them, not nearly as gracefully, bashing my head against a giant column.

Everything goes dark for a moment, but then slowly, the majestic ceiling comes back into soft focus.

"It sifts from leaden sieves,
It powders all the wood,
It fills with alabaster wool
The wrinkles of the road," I whisper.

"Hey . . ." Kit nudges me with his sneaker.

"Is he all right?" Darryl asks.

Maria leans over me. "His eyes are dilated."

"He's fine." Shy offers me a hand. I grasp on and she pulls me up. "Emily Dickinson, right?" she says as an aside.

"I said that out loud?" I rub my head.

She shoots me a look I can't decipher. She's probably thinking what a pretentious ass I am, but that's the least of my problems right now.

As we explore the vast space, it feels like our lights are growing dimmer, but it's the space that's expanding, swallowing up our light in big, heaving gulps.

"I don't remember seeing anything like this from the guidebook," I say, trying to pull myself back together.

"What if we discovered a whole new cave system?" Kit gawks at the scenery. "Maybe they'll name it after us. Or me, really. Kit's Cave. Has the best ring to it."

"You can have it," Shy says, flinching away from a dripping stalactite. "I hate this place."

Darryl paces the floor like that deranged polar bear at the zoo they had to put down. "Grant's reciting poetry, Kit's lost in some Santa fantasy. Does anyone want to snap back to reality, because I'd really like to get out of here."

"Aw . . . is someone getting hungwy?" Kit says in a whiny voice, rubbing his eyes like a crying baby.

Darryl takes a swipe at him, but Kit's too fast.

"You guys, come on," Shy says as she stands in front of an enormous stretch of rock dividing the center of the cavern. "We need to decide. Stick to the right tunnel or the left."

"Anyone have a coin?" Kit says.

As everyone's digging in their pockets, a tremendous gust of air rushes over us, making Shy's ponytail sway.

"Please tell me you guys felt that," she says.

"What the . . ." Darryl shines his light up the stone wall, focusing in on a wide slit above.

"Air is good," Kit says as he climbs up, shining his flashlight inside the gap. "That's got to be coming from the surface."

"Possibly," I say as I climb up to peek inside. "But caves can be deceptive. A sound you hear could be miles away or right over your shoulder. Same with air. It could be coming from the surface or it could just be pressure forcing the air to move. Caves take in air and push it out. Like breath."

"That's not at all creepy," Kit says as he climbs inside the opening. "This thing is endless, but it's only about three feet high. We'd have to crawl."

"I know how to crawl." Darryl lights up. "I've been working on it."

Everyone looks at him like maybe he's the one losing it now.

"I know Maria's a ballbuster," Kit laughs, "but—"

"For basic training, you sickos," he says defensively. "The key is to use your forearms instead of your elbows, but there's no avoiding the knees."

Another gust of air comes through and Kit grins back at us. "I think we should go for it. What do we have to lose?"

"I don't know . . . our lives?" Maria places her hands on her hips.

"Kit's right," I say as I check out the other tunnels. "I don't feel air in either one of these."

"On that show *Legends and Myths* . . ." Darryl runs his hand over the rock face. "They said the natives thought caves were sleeping giants. So I guess we're basically going to be crawling down the giant's throat."

"On that note," Kit says as he hops down and places his hand on my shoulder. "I think Grant should take the lead on this one. He's got the best light."

"Yeah, okay," I say, trying to swallow my nerves. Ever since the incident I've had issues with confined spaces, which is funny, considering where I am now. But this was never part of the plan. I should be dead by now.

As I'm making sure my pack is secure, I swear I hear that wordless whisper. It could just be the air moving through the slit in the rock, but it feels like something more.

I'm staring into the dark, toward the boulder choke, when Shy steps in front of me.

"What do you keep looking for? Are you expecting someone?"

"It's nothing."

"Sure," she answers. But I can tell by the way she's looking at me that she knows I'm lying.

Climbing up to the gap, I shove my pack in first and then crawl inside the crevice.

The strange breeze pushes against me. To Kit, it might feel like an invitation, but to me, it feels ominous, like it doesn't want us to come in. And we have no idea what's on the other end of this. Could be a huge drop or could narrow to a point we can't get through. And backing out of this thing would be a nightmare, at best.

The stone is wet and cold, and the air is more humid in here, if that's even possible. As I inch forward, I realize what it reminds me of: a coffin.

I'm trying not to make any contact with the stone ceiling above me, but it's impossible to avoid. Every time it skims across my spine, I'm reminded of how trapped I feel.

As I move forward, I hear them behind me, joking around, laughing. It should put me at ease, knowing they're here with me, but it only makes me feel more alone.

A tremendous roar of crushing stone permeates the atmosphere; I freeze in place.

"That sounds like the boulder choke," Darryl says.

"Maybe it's a rescue team," Maria whispers. "Should we go back?"

"It's probably just the rocks settling," Shy says. "We have to keep moving. If it's a rescue team, they'll find us."

As much as I try to bar the thought from my head, I can't help wondering if it's the person who's been following me, coming for justice.

And just like that, everything I've done, everything I came down here for, comes crashing over me again.

Grinding my knees into the rock, I keep pressing forward, but it feels like I'm trudging through glue. My breath is coming in short bursts now—at least I think it's my breath. I stop to listen, but all I hear is the pounding of my heart, thrumming in my ear drums, like a wet hammer.

Laying my cheek against the cold wet stone, I feel the rock pressing in on me. Even the air going in and out of my body feels poisonous, like it's clinging to the inside of my lungs, choking me from the inside out.

"Hey," Shy says, shoving my foot.

I want to get up. I want to keep moving, but my body won't let me. It feels like I'm welded to the stone.

"What's wrong?" She wedges in next to me, lying down flat so she can look me in my eyes.

I try to answer, but nothing comes out. Not even air.

"Breathe," she whispers. "Breathe with me. You're fine.

You're just having a panic attack. My grandma has these all the time. Inhale nice and slow and then exhale."

Locking in on her deep brown eyes, I breathe in time with her. And I get the strangest feeling we've been here before. Just like this. Maybe in another life. Or maybe I really am losing it.

I'm moving my mouth, but no sound is coming out.

"Listen to me. Whatever you're hiding, whatever you came down here for . . . that's your business. But you said you'd get us out of here and I'm not going to let you give up. On us. On yourself. You have to keep moving. For better or worse, we're stuck with each other. The only way we can get through this is if we work together."

"You're not making out, are you?" Kit calls from behind.

"What's the holdup?" Darryl asks.

"I don't like it in here," Maria chimes in.

"It's like we're in a rock sandwich," Kit says.

Darryl sighs. "Will you *please* stop talking about food."

"I'm sorry. I'm starving. I could eat a rock sandwich right about now. As long as it had ketchup. Ketchup is the king of all condiments."

I hear a stomach growl. "Now look what you've done," Darryl yells.

With tears streaming down my face, I let out an exhausted laugh.

"Ready?" Shy asks.

I nod.

Prying myself off the floor, I move. One step at a time.

I can feel her with me. All of them, pushing me forward.

And for the first time in a very long while, I'm grateful.

15

THE crawl gradually opens up, leading us to yet another empty cavern, but it's not empty at all. There are mammoth columns of calcite deposits and strange ribbon formations dangling from the ceiling. When you shine your light on them, you can see right through them. It reminds me of being under water, exploring a coral reef in the Bahamas. Even the air feels wrong, like breathing through a respirator. But unlike the ocean, there's no sign of sunlight beaming from above. No hope of kicking to the surface, coming up for air.

I may not deserve to crawl out of this cave, but they do.

As I grasp onto a pillar of rock to pull my aching body to a standing position, a strange breeze circles around my head, the faintest whisper. I turn, shining my light down the narrow chute from where we just came. There are footprints. But none of us could walk in there. Stepping closer, I'm shocked to find the prints are deep red. The unmistakable color of blood.

Shy steps next to me.

"Do you see that?" I whisper, my skin prickling up in goose bumps. "Someone's following us."

"It's just your knees," she says with a raised brow, before walking off.

I look down and, sure enough, there's blood seeping through my pants. I must've been grinding my knees into the stone harder than I thought. Pulling the synthetic cloth away from the wounds, I shake it off and join the others, but I can't stop looking behind me.

"How do we even know we're going the right way?" Maria asks as we trudge forward.

"Do you see another way?" Kit asks.

"I don't even care as long as we can walk upright, like humans," Darryl says as he tries to stretch out his back.

"But what if we're just going deeper?"

"Grant, what was that you were saying about the water marks?" Darryl asks.

"Earth to Grant." Kit covers his mouth, making it sound like it's coming from an old radio.

"Sorry." I turn back around, forcing myself to stay grounded in the present. "These tunnels were formed by water," I say, running my hand over the scallop-shaped indentations in the stone. "Millions of years of water needling its way through limestone. Think of it like a giant block of Jarlsberg."

"Jarlsberg?" Kit asks.

"It's a fancy name for cheese," Shy answers, clearly annoyed by my analogy. "Swiss cheese. The one with holes in it."

"Man, I wish this place really was made out of cheese." Kit sighs. "We could eat our way out of here. Right, Darryl?"

"What are you getting at?" Darryl snaps. "For your info, I don't even like swiss cheese."

"You need to chill out on that. Stop being so sensitive. We've all been teased before," Kit says. "I'm trash. You're fat. Maria's hoochie. Shy's manly."

"Manly?"

"And what do you mean, 'hoochie'?"

"So you *do* think I'm fat."

"Hey . . . whoa," Kit raises his hands in the air. "I'm just saying. I bet even Grant the fifth here has taken some shade."

They all look back at me, and I know I have to give them something. I don't need Shy to be any more suspicious of me than she already is.

"Neat freak," I say.

"What, like your clothes folded a certain way?"

"No. Like my toothbrush . . . it has to be facing west."

"Why?"

I take in a steeling breath. "To catch the sunlight so it can kill the bacteria."

They all stare at me for a second, like I just spoke an entirely different language, and then start cracking up.

"That's not a real problem," Shy says. "That's just somebody with way too much time on their hands."

"You shouldn't make fun of him," Maria says. "It's OCD. It's a real thing."

"Okay." Shy shakes her head. "Well, you can come over and organize my stuff anytime."

"Maybe I will," I say, which I immediately want to take back.

"You wish." She gives me a look—a cross between disdain and disbelief—before pushing past everyone to take the lead.

"Don't make me fight you," Kit says over his shoulder.

"I didn't mean anything. I swear, I think I have a fever," I try to explain. "And I had no idea you and Shy were . . ."

"A thing?" He raises a brow. "Not my type. Not by a long shot. Wrong equipment."

"Oh," I say, way more surprised than I wanted to sound.

"It's all right." He slows down, so we can talk. "People used to think that all the time about me and Shy, and I let them. It was easier than the truth. Especially in our neighborhood. But rumors do what they do, and one day I just got sick of denying them."

"That must've been tough," I say, thinking of Bennett, of what his family would do if he told them the truth.

"The buildup was the worst part. Worrying all the time about what people would think, how they'd treat me. If

I'd get beat up . . . or worse. But nothing really happened." He ducks under a jagged piece of rock. "I'm the same person I've always been. Just gay."

I look ahead at Shy and Maria, locked arm in arm, talking quietly. She's probably telling Maria what a giant douche I am. And maybe she's right.

"Wondering what Shy's type is?" Kit asks with a knowing smile.

"No." I jut my head back. "You've got me all wrong."

"Well, I'm not even sure Shy has a type."

"What do you mean?"

"So you *are* interested." He grins up at me.

"I'm not interested *or* disinterested. Just making conversation."

"Grant, Grant, Grant . . ." He shakes his head and places his hand on my shoulder. "I'll give you the lowdown. Back in middle school, she liked the same things as me. Drake. Maybe a little Zac Efron on the side. Guys try all the time with her, but Shy's got her hands full with training and taking care of her grandma."

"What's wrong with her grandma?"

"Alzheimer's."

"Hold up," Shy calls back, stopping the group. "Do you guys hear that?"

I freeze in place, quieting my breath. That dark feeling seeps right back into my pores. The whisper. Can they hear it?

"It sounds like rushing water. A lot of it," Kit says as he slips to the front. "Maybe it's a way out."

Before I can even tell him that we need to be cautious, that there might be someone else down here, Kit's running ahead.

My pulse is pounding as I go after him, and my throat's bone dry. If something happens to him . . .

But when he reaches the jagged opening where the sound's coming from, he covers his mouth and staggers back in horror, sinking against the cave wall.

16

EVERYONE rushes forward, afraid to see what's around the corner . . . afraid not to.

But it's not the scenery that has Kit clasping his hand over his mouth, gasping for air. It's the smell. It's beyond foul. Ammonia and dirt and rot. The odor's so intense that we're all gagging on it. I try not to breathe too deeply, but the scent seems to cling to the inside of my nostrils. Despite the stench, I'm happy to see that it's just us. If there really was someone else down here, I'm pretty sure I would've seen them by now. They would've made themselves known. I need to get that out of my head.

Shining my light over the basketball court–size cavern, there's four huge plates of rock balanced above us at precarious angles. The ceiling must've shifted during the collapse. I see an opening on the far end, but in order to get there we're going to have to navigate through a maze of strange-looking mounds of dirt.

"What are those?" Maria asks.

"Forget that." Darryl squints into the dark. "What's making that sound?"

Beyond the pungent odor, there's a strange chittering sound, almost like something sizzling in a pan.

I focus my headlamp on one of the mysterious mounds of dirt. From the ground to the tip of the taper it's got to be sixteen feet tall. In the glow of the LED light, the mound glistens like polished onyx. As I step forward, trying to figure out what makes it shine that way, I see that the mound is moving.

My stomach lurches. "Guano," I whisper.

"Gua–what?" Kit asks.

"Didn't you watch *Scooby-Doo*?" Darryl's mouth gapes open. "It's bat crap."

"Crap doesn't make that sound," Kit says.

"Yeah . . . about that . . ." I let out a measured breath. "That's the cockroaches . . . *eating* the bat crap."

"Gua-no freaking way," Kit says as he starts to back up. "We'll find another tunnel."

"Wait." I shine my light on the partially collapsed ceiling and then to the craggy opening on the other side. "This is good. This is exactly where we want to be."

"I don't know what you're into," Kit says, "but if you think I'm eating that . . . you're crazier than I thought."

"No." I shake my head. "If there's guano . . . there's bats."

"Uh . . . yeah, I'm not eating bats, either. Do I look like Ozzy damn Osbourne to you?"

"Not to eat." I can't help but crack a smile. "Bats hang out near openings; they leave the caves at night to feed. Since this is collapsed, they must've gone off searching for a way out. If we find the bats . . ." I lock eyes with Shy. "We find the way out. They can lead us to the surface."

Shy pans her flashlight over the cavern and then gives a slight nod. "Fine."

"You want to walk . . . through *there*," Kit says, "through piles of bat crap and cockroaches and who knows what else?"

"Unless you have the power of flight," Shy says as she yanks down his hood, "that's exactly what's going to happen."

"Hey, look at this." Darryl reaches down into the muck, pulling something out.

Maria shines her light on it. "It's a pocket watch, one of those really old ones with the chains."

"This is awesome, right?" He wipes it off on his jeans. "It means someone's been down here before."

"Yeah, like a hundred years ago," Kit says, staring at the black sludge covering the cave floor. "I wonder if the rest of him is in there, too?"

Darryl shrugs. "Finders, keepers."

As Darryl slips it in his pocket, Kit wrinkles up his nose. "See, now that's just nasty."

"How am I even going to do this?" Maria winces as she shines her flashlight over the path. "I don't want to kill any of them."

"She has a thing about that." Darryl shoots me a look of apology. "She thinks it's bad karma to kill any living thing."

I have to look away. I can only imagine what Maria will think of me when she figures out who I really am.

"Piggyback," Darryl says as he leans down. "That way, if I step on any of them, it will be on me . . . not you."

"That's why you're the sweetest," Maria says as she hops on his back and kisses him on the cheek.

"Slow and steady," Darryl says as he starts walking across, but the sound of the roaches crunching beneath the soles of his boots only seems to agitate the horde, making them sizzle even louder.

Shy stands next to me, her eyes trained straight ahead. "Are you sure about the bats? You really think we can find them?"

"It's the best lead we have." I shove my hands in my pockets, mostly to warm them up, but also because I don't want her to see how nervous I am. "I know we have our differences, but I want you to know that I'm going to do everything I can to get you out of here."

"You better." There's an edge to her voice, but when I look at her, there's no real anger in her wide brown eyes. Maybe fear, mixed with sadness? Resignation. That's the word I'm looking for. I want to ask her why she hates me so much, but I'm not sure I want to know. Wouldn't matter anyway.

When Darryl and Maria reach the other side, they give the thumbs-up.

Kit is panting, hopping around in place, clearly trying to psych himself up. "I'm just doing it," he says as he takes off running across the cavern, leaping over boulders, weaving through the mounds like a professional football player. I want to yell at him to slow down, but that could cause this whole place to come down, and also it's hard to be mad at someone like Kit. There's something about him. You can't help but like him.

With all three of them safely on the other side, I turn to Shy. "Ladies first."

She shoots me a withering look. "Then you better get moving."

"Suit yourself," I say as I crouch to make sure my boots are tied, but mostly it's to hide the flush I feel taking over my face. As soon as the worst of it passes, I get up and start making my way to the other side. I'm trying to take it slow, but when I feel the cockroaches squirming beneath me I want to take Kit's approach and get it over with as quick as possible. Knowing my luck, I'd probably end up tripping and diving headfirst into one of those guano piles.

As soon as I'm safe on the other side, I signal to Shy.

She starts casually walking toward us, stepping on the cockroaches as if it doesn't bother her in the least.

Maria's gagging. "Can you at least *try* not to kill them?"

"What'd I tell you . . ." Kit says. "She's an animal."

"Maybe she's just imagining stomping on Grant's head," Darryl chuckles.

"Darryl!" Maria smacks him in the chest.

"What? It's a joke."

"Don't pay any attention to him." Maria rolls her eyes. "And that's just Shy. She's hard to get to know. She'll warm up once she trusts you."

"But she's got the best BS detector I've ever seen," Kit says.

"Seriously." Darryl crosses his arms over his chest. "Forget the Olympics. She should be an interrogator."

"As long as you're real, she'll be cool with you." Kit shoots me a look. "But if you try to hide something from her . . . forget it."

"Come on, Shy. Cut the act," Darryl calls out. "You're not freaked out by thousands of cockroaches?"

"Please," she replies. "I work at Papa John's."

"What?" Kit's voice raises about two octaves. "Is that the reason you're always giving me free pizza?"

Shy starts to say something, no doubt some stinging comeback, when a pile of guano collapses right in front of her, sending cockroaches scrambling for purchase.

I'm getting ready to tell her to go around, when I see the strangest look come over her. With a shallow breath, she asks, "They're on me . . . aren't they?"

I skim my headlamp down her neck, her chest, her hips, and then stop. Her light-blue track pants are covered in shiny, black, skittering roaches.

Everyone's yelling at her to run, but she just stands there, paralyzed.

It starts low, the grumble beneath our feet, until I can feel the entire cavern begin to tremble.

I spring forward to get her, struggling to pick her up over my shoulder. As I'm trying to run, I feel the cockroach carpet moving beneath my feet, the cavern crumbling behind us. And all I can think is that I don't want to die like this, buried in here with whoever owned that watch, cockroaches feeding on our flesh.

We make it to the other side just as the cavern completely collapses, sending a huge rush of foul air whooshing through the tunnel.

"I don't care if you have to bludgeon me to death," Shy screams, "just get them off me."

I set her down and we all start beating the cockroaches off of her. Even Maria gets in on it, cursing up a storm as she stomps away. So much for bad karma.

"Enough." Shy cowers. "That's enough."

We stand there in silence, roach carcasses strewn all around us. Shy's leaning over, bracing her hands against her knees, when I see her shoulders begin to shake. At first I think she's crying, but when she looks up I see the huge grin taking over her face. With her eyes squeezed shut, she begins to laugh. Something about seeing her like that, this serious girl cracking up like that, makes me join in. Soon everyone's dying laughing. The sound is earsplitting, but it only makes us laugh harder. I don't know if we're just delirious or relieved, but, in this moment, it's the funniest thing that's ever happened to me. Maybe to any of us.

As we're stumbling forward, trying to catch our breath, Kit's flashlight flickers a few times before burning out.

"Come on . . . don't do this." He slaps it against the palm of his hand.

"Does anyone have extra batteries?" Shy asks with a strange urgency to her voice.

"No." I shake my head. "But this is a good reminder. We should probably only use one flashlight at a time from here on out."

"Are you crazy?" Darryl says. "It's hella dark down here."

"We should be okay with my headlamp and one flashlight. We need to conserve batteries."

"He's right," Shy says.

I'm a little surprised she's agreeing with me on something, but I'm not complaining.

Kit grips Shy's arm. "I can't do the dark. You know that. I just can't," he says, sheer panic making his voice tremble. "I *need* my flashlight."

"You can carry mine," Darryl says.

"No. I need *this* one."

Shy places her hand against his cheek. "It's okay, I'm not going to let anything happen to you."

As far as I can tell, it's just a cheap red plastic flashlight, probably from the dollar store, but then I notice he's got his name written on it in thick black marker. *Property of Kit Jackson*. This is something more than just being scared of the dark.

"How about we switch the batteries out," I suggest.

"See?" Shy says as she pries the dead one out of his hands and quickly replaces the batteries from Darryl's. "No harm done."

"You can lead the way," I add as she hands it back to him.

"Yeah . . . yeah," he says as he stares into the warm glow, slowly regaining his composure. "That could be cool."

Shy gives me a quick look of thanks before she remembers that I disgust her. I'm not saying she's wrong, but I wonder what she sees in me. If she sees a monster.

As Maria and Shy turn off their flashlights and we continue forward, I feel a shift in the atmosphere. Maybe it's just the dark, or the cramped quarters getting to us, but it's more than losing a light. It's a reminder that time is running out. Eventually, all the batteries will burn out, and if we can't find a way out of here before that happens, we'll burn out right along with them.

17

BATTERED and filthy, we trudge forward, cavern after cavern, tunnel after tunnel, dead end after dead end.

I'm not sure what everyone else is thinking, but Kit doesn't even bother charging ahead anymore. Darryl and Maria are starting to pick at each other. And Shy hasn't said another word since Kit's light burned out.

All it would take is a tiny pinprick of sunlight. Anything to let us know that we're on the right track. That it's going to be okay.

I keep looking around for something familiar, anything I might remember from the guidebook, but it all looks the same to me now. The hollowed-out spaces, the towering columns, and delicate formations that I once thought of as beautiful look ugly to me now.

There's no sign of the bats. No sign of life.

Except for the water trickling down the walls. It almost hurts to think about it. That water's coming from the surface. For all we know, it could be right above our heads, but we can't reach it. It's like the cave keeps opening up to us in layers and all we can do at this point is trust that it wants to lead us out. I know that sounds crazy, thinking of it like that, but the more time I spend down here, the more it feels like a living, breathing thing, with lungs and a heart . . . a will of its own.

A huge drop of water falls from the ceiling, sliding down my neck. They call it a cave kiss, but it feels like an assault. The constant drip reminds me of the grandfather clock in our foyer. On the face, there's a sun and a moon rotating in phases. How many suns and moons have passed since we've been down here? It's impossible to gauge time down here, but it feels like weeks. I wonder if my family knows what happened. If they're trying to find a way to get to me or if they're secretly relieved.

But then my thoughts turn to my sister. How I've left her alone to deal with this . . . to deal with *them*. It seemed like the best solution, but now it feels like the most selfish thing I've ever done. And that's really saying something.

That's why I needed this to go as smoothly as possible, why I planned everything to the letter, because I didn't want to give myself the time to go soft, time to sit and stew on everything that brought me here. And the more time I spend with these people, the more confused I become about everything. A part of me wants to just sneak off and bail. I'm good at that. But I can't escape the fact that I'm the reason they're stuck down here in the first place. I have to get them out of here. Because the alternative is too grim to even contemplate.

I don't want to be the first to give in, but I'm stumbling over my own feet at this point, and what little visibility I have is playing tricks on me.

Every once in a while, I get flashes, shadows in my peripheral, making me think there's someone behind me. I know it's not real. It can't be. I'm the last one in line. Even if someone was deranged enough to follow me down here, I doubt they would've survived the collapse, let alone made it past the boulder choke or the caved-in guano cavern. It's probably just the rocks settling. The acoustics playing tricks on my senses. But no matter how hard I try to convince myself it's just fatigue, the dark getting to me, I can't shake it. If I close my eyes, I swear I can feel the whisper breathing down my neck. Closer . . . and closer . . .

I swallow hard, gathering the nerve to look behind me. As soon as I turn my head, something pushes me, or my knees give out—whatever it is, I go crashing to the cold stone floor.

When I open my eyes, they're all gathered around, staring down at me.

"He's still breathing."

"He needs water."

They press the water bottle to my cracked lips and I

drink. It tastes like pure mud sliding down my throat, but it's exactly what I need. I'm trying to figure out how I'm going to get back on my feet, when Shy lets out a heavy sigh, sinking against the wall. "This seems like as good a place as any to rest."

And I know exactly what she means. As miserable a place as any. No matter where we go, how far we walk, it's the same. Cold. Dark. Damp. Unforgiving.

As everyone finds a place to sit, Kit starts going through my pack. Normally, it would make me crazy, watching someone mess around with my stuff like that, but I'm too tired to care. Pushing aside all the ropes and carabiners, he pulls out a silver pouch. "*Recovery bag*. What's this for?"

"It's part of the emergency kit, to help you get warm. Try it."

I can tell he's interested, but he shakes his head. "I'm not getting in anything that looks like one of those hot dog wrappers down at Fas Mart. If something comes at us down here and I've got to run, you won't see me hopping around in that thing looking like a tasty treat."

I know he's probably just making a joke out of it, but I wonder if he feels it, too . . . like there's something down here with us. Watching.

"You should use it." Shy grabs it, tossing it over to me.

"Thanks," I say as I try to unfold it, but my hands are still trembling.

"It's more for me than you. Anything to get your teeth to stop chattering."

As she's helping me get into it, I say, "You know, skin on skin is the quickest way to warm up."

"Not gonna happen," she answers, but at least I finally got a genuine smile out of her.

Pulling the bag around my shoulders, I start breathing hot air into it.

"Shivering is good," Maria says. "It's when you stop being cold that you have to worry. That's the second phase of hypothermia."

"Remember that homeless guy you had to treat, down by the canals? They had to cut off his toes because of frostbite."

"Babe." Maria looks at him with wide eyes.

"What?" he says. "It's true."

"Thanks for the uplifting bedtime story." Shy glares at him.

"What's this?" Kit asks as he holds up a puffy manila envelope with "Grant" written on the front in perfect cursive.

I know that writing; it belongs to my mother. But I was meticulous about packing for this trip. There's no way I would've overlooked something like that . . . But then I remember the envelope in her robe pocket, how strange she was acting when I saw her in the hallway before I left. She must've slipped it in when she was pretending to adjust my straps.

I rip it open and find four packets of freeze-dried food. Just thinking about her doing something like this for me, in secret, makes my throat tight, like I can barely swallow.

"What's up, dude?" Darryl asks. "You look like you just saw a ghost."

"It's from my mom," I say as I sink into the dark for a few seconds' reprieve. "She must've slipped this in my bag before I left."

"What is it?" Kit asks as he continues to dig through the bag. "More first aid stuff?"

I pull out the packets. "It's food."

Everyone drops what they're doing and presses in.

Shy studies me. "I thought you weren't allowed to have food on this trip."

"I wasn't." I glance up at her.

"Please tell me it's beef jerky . . . or granola bars," Darryl says.

Maria looks at him in shock. "You hate granola bars."

"Not anymore." He clasps his hands in front of him. "I love them, and all of their chalky, grainy goodness."

"It's better than that." I smile. "Beef Stroganoff. Chicken pot pie. Mac and cheese. And one packet of Neapolitan ice cream."

Maria inspects one of the bags. "I think this stuff has gone bad. It's all hard."

"It's freeze-dried," I say.

"Wait. Is this astronaut food?" Darryl asks. "The same stuff they eat up in space?"

"Basically."

"Can we have some?" he asks, licking his lips.

"Of course."

After a very heated debate on what to eat first, we finally decide on the chicken pot pie. Adding water to the pouch, we shake it up and pass it around. We don't have anything to eat it with, so we just take turns sipping it out of the bag. It's cold and slimy, but my God, it tastes so good. I know everyone's starving, but we manage to make it last, passing it around more times than I thought possible.

"Remind me to give your mom a huge hug when we get out of here," Kit says.

"Yeah . . . that's not really her thing."

"Hugging?" Maria asks.

I pull the recovery bag up under my chin.

"That's all my family does," she says. "It's suffocating." Maria picks at her blue nail polish. "But right now, I'd do anything to see them."

Everyone's quiet, and I know we're all thinking the same thing. Wondering if we'll ever see our families again. The mistakes we've made. What we'd do differently.

"Your mom can't be that bad if she snuck this in your bag," Kit says.

I pull my knees to my chest. "I can't stop thinking about the last time I saw her. She was standing in the hallway on the second floor, where the nursery used to be."

"Did she turn it into a huge closet?" Maria asks. "I always wanted one of those."

"No. Nothing like that." I stare off into the darkness. "They just plastered over the door."

"Why would you waste a perfectly good room?" Darryl asks. "Did you have asbestos or something?"

"No." I take in a shallow breath. "I had a little brother. David." It feels good to say his name. "He only lived for about six weeks. But when he died, she just sealed it off and never spoke of him again."

A heavy silence permeates the space between us.

"I lost a brother too," Maria says quietly.

Darryl smooths his hand over her knee.

"I get it," Maria continues, her eyes glassy. "Sometimes I wish I could forget. But his picture's everywhere. They didn't even get rid of his clothes. So not only do I have to deal with the memories in my head, I have to see him everywhere I turn." She wipes away a tear slipping down her cheek. "Maybe your mom had it right. Life is for the living, you know."

I nod, tears prickling the back of my eyes. "My mom's always been strong. A lot stronger than me. Than any of us, really. Except maybe Mare."

"Mare?" Shy asks.

"My sister, Meredith." I smile through my quivering chin. "You'd like her. She's a lot more fun than me."

"No offense," Kit says with a burst of uncomfortable laughter, "but that wouldn't be very hard."

"None taken." I grin.

Darryl's stomach lets out an angry growl. "The beast has awoken."

Maria slaps his stomach.

"No, but seriously . . ." He shifts his weight. "When can we eat again?"

Kit picks up the remaining pouches. "So, if we have three packages left and they're about five hundred calories each, that's fifteen hundred divided between us. What's your BMR?" he asks Darryl.

"I don't know."

"Just do 9.99 times your weight, plus 6.25 times your height, minus 4.92 times your age and add five."

"Yeah, right." Darryl laughs.

Shy grabs the packages, shoving them in the backpack. "All we need to know is that we have to make it last, just in case . . ."

"In case of what?" Darryl asks.

We all exchange looks.

"In case it takes a little longer than we think to find a way out," Maria says, way too cheerfully.

Desperate for a subject change, I nudge Kit with my knee. "So, you're good at math."

"A little too good." Shy glares at him.

"I don't get it."

"Don't mind her," Kit replies nonchalantly. "She's still upset about my little brush with the law."

"There wasn't anything little about it." Shy sits up extra straight, like she's ready to pounce. "You were running a gambling ring."

"Just fun and games." Kit smiles.

"Not when you're counting cards. Cheating people."

"High yield, low risk." He winks at me.

"Not low enough," Maria murmurs.

"Look, it was my first offense. I got off on probation."

"Which means if you don't straighten up, you'll be going to jail," Shy says. "You're better than that."

"You should go to business school," I say.

"Oh yeah?" Kit asks. "With what money?"

"There's scholarships."

"Not for people like me."

I think about how easy it was for everyone I know to get into college. We didn't think of it as a privilege. It was just another hoop we had to jump through to appease our parents. Stay on track. The track to what, I'm not so sure about, but Kit deserved that same opportunity.

"Maybe I can help with that."

He looks me up and down. "Unless you're some secret Richie Rich, I don't see how. Besides, even if I had the money, the grades, I still wouldn't be able to get in anywhere decent."

"Why? You're clearly smart enough."

"And I'm also a felon now."

I can't help thinking about how unfair it is that I get a clean record while Kit will be marked with this forever, and over something so small in comparison to what I did.

"There are ways around that," I say. "Maybe I can help with that, too . . . or my father can."

"I knew it." Darryl sits up straight. "Does your dad work for the government?"

"Sort of."

"High-ranking military?" He scoots closer. "Because that's my plan, you know. Marines. I'll have structure, get in shape, help people . . . all the things you're always talking to me about," he says as he looks at Maria. "And I like America. Yeah, it's messed up right now, but maybe I can make a difference."

"You can make a difference . . . *here* . . . with me." Maria cuddles against his arm. "I don't want you getting blown up."

"But then you can put me back together again. It's perfect." Darryl kisses her on the cheek and she sinks further into him. "Maybe your dad could put in a good word for me, too . . . pull some strings?"

"Yeah, it won't hurt to ask," I say, shocked to find myself talking about the future in any capacity.

"You can cut the act," Shy says. "I know exactly who you are."

I'm not sure what my face is doing, but it feels like my insides are being carved out. I let out a deep sigh, bracing myself for impact, but it's almost a relief.

"We went to the tree-lighting ceremony this year."

"That was right before . . ." My voice trails off. I still can't even say it out loud.

"Before what?" She gives me a puzzled look, but there's no anger in her voice, no fear.

And I realize she still hasn't put it together. "Nothing." I swallow hard.

"Wait . . . did you guys hook up or something?" Darryl asks.

"No." She looks disgusted by the idea. "His dad's our senator. Senator Tavish."

"No way." Darryl's eyes light up. "I knew it."

"Your dad's the senator?" Maria says, more as a statement than a question.

"Yeah." I pull the heat bag up to my nose, wishing I could disappear inside of it. I'm waiting for one of them to figure it out, but it never seems to click.

"Why didn't you tell us?" Kit jumps to his feet, hitting his head against the rock ceiling. "That seems like key information. Like . . . *Hey,*" he says, rubbing his head, *"my dad's famous."*

"Doesn't matter," Shy says curtly. "We're all trapped. We're all equals down here."

"Yeah . . . but if he's the senator's son, we're going to get rescued, for sure. Maybe they don't give a crap about us, but him? He's our golden ticket."

"Please tell me you're not going to start talking about Willy Wonka again?" Shy groans.

"He's obsessed with that book," Maria says as she puts on a coat of lip balm.

"Yeah, when that's your *only* book, you kind of get attached to it," Kit says as he settles back down.

I'm embarrassed to think about my shelves at home. Hundreds of books I've never even thought about picking up. Leather bound—all the classics. I even cut into a few of them to make a stash for my weed.

"Man, I bet you have access to all kinds of top secret information," Darryl says. "Roswell. Blue Bean."

"It's not really like that. All my dad does is shake hands,

attend meetings . . . occasionally he votes on whatever his party tells him to vote on. He's a puppet. Nothing more."

"Ouch," Kit says.

"Don't get me wrong, he's a good guy, but sometimes I wonder if he just followed in our ancestors' footsteps out of duty to the family name, not because it's what he wanted. He was never given a choice. Like when he talks about this trip, how it was the best time of his life, I wonder if he thought about disappearing . . . about never going back."

Shy looks at me and I know she's wondering if that was my plan as well.

Darryl scratches the stubble on his chin. "I never thought about money like that. Being a trap."

"That's kind of sad," Maria says. "Your dad always looks so happy on TV."

I crack a smile. "He's happy as long as he gets his Scotch in the evenings . . . time for his ducks . . ."

"Ducks?"

"Is that some rich slang?" Kit asks.

"No." I let out a soft laugh. "Ducks. Like *quack quack*."

"What, for pets?"

"He carves them out of white cedar and paints them."

"Like a hobby," Maria says. "That's nice."

"It's not nice," I try to explain. "He makes them super realistic, so he can attract *real* ducks."

"To take pictures of them?"

"To shoot them."

Maria mutters something under her breath.

"Like Peking duck?" Kit grins.

Darryl's stomach growls. "Dude, come on."

"No." I shake my head, sinking farther into the bag. "He doesn't even eat them. Sometimes he'll have the prettiest ones stuffed, the males, but most of the time he just gives them to the locals."

"Ah . . . the poor folk," Shy says, raising her eyebrows. "How generous."

"You know what's funny?" Kit stretches out his spindly legs. "They're probably looking at that dead duck like *What the hell am I supposed to do with this?*"

Everyone starts cracking up, and I can't help joining in. Maybe it's lack of sleep, lack of food, but this is the most I've laughed in I don't even know how long. And how pathetic is that?

A strange whisper pulls my attention.

"Did you hear that?" Darryl asks.

My skin explodes in goose bumps. I want to tell him no, but I hear it all the time now. It seems to be getting closer.

"Besides roaches and bats . . ." Kit shines the flashlight on the wet stone surrounding us. "What else could be living down here?"

"Snakes? Lizards?" I reply.

"What about people?" Darryl says as he handles the pocket watch he found, nervously opening and closing the hinged cover.

"Whoever left that is long gone by now," Kit says.

"What if it's his ghost?" Darryl raises his brows.

"Cut it out, man. It's bad enough."

"No . . . but seriously . . . hear me out. They say fugitives come down here to hide. Murderers. This one guy killed like nine—"

"I've heard the story," I interrupt, "but that was way down in the cave system, not anywhere near the tourist part."

"Do you see any lights? Any handrails?" Kit says. "I'm pretty sure we're as far off the grid as you can get."

I shine my light into the tunnel behind us, but the darkness devours it.

"Hey," Kit says. "You've been spooked since we found you. Not just about the collapse. What is it? What aren't you telling us?"

I can feel Shy staring at me. I'm struggling to come up with a response, when Darryl unwittingly rescues me.

"You guys . . . what if there's something *else* down here?" His eyes light up. "Another life form . . . something that hasn't even been discovered yet . . . *aliens*."

Shy, Kit, and Maria simultaneously pick up whatever's around them and chuck it at him.

"I'm serious." He tries and fails to duck out of the way. "The government . . . this is where they'd hide stuff like that. This whole place could be an underground testing facility. Didn't any of you guys watch *Lost*?"

"You watch way too much TV."

"It could be in our heads," I tell him, but I'm also telling it to myself. "The biggest enemy down here isn't the cold or starvation or even the dangers of the cave. The real enemy is the dark. There's a caving term for it. They call it the rapture. It's when you see things . . . hear things . . ."

"Guantanamo," Darryl whispers. We turn to look at him, his face almost gaunt in the dim light. "They use sensory deprivation to torture people. One detainee scratched his own eyes out, trying to find the pins of light he kept seeing in the back of his eyes."

"I get that," Kit says as he messes with the string on his hoodie. "I hate the dark."

Everyone gets extremely quiet and I know this has something to do with Kit's freak-out back there, when his light burned out.

"Have you had that flashlight for a long time?" I ask.

"Yeah," he says, absently running his thumb over his name. "Since I was six. This police lady gave it to me at the hospital. I know it's dumb, but it's kind of like a security blanket, I guess."

I instantly feel bad for even bringing it up. "Hey, you don't have to talk about it if you don't–"

"My first fosters were nice," he says. "I mean, I don't remember anything bad, so they must've been okay. But some people just like the babies. As soon as you start talking, moving around too much, it's on to the next one. And that next one wasn't so good for me. Whenever I got in trouble, which was a lot, they'd lock me in one of those old steamer trunks. It smelled like tobacco and old paper, but it wasn't the worst way to spend a few hours. At least I knew I was safe from the other kids. There was this one kid, Ronny. He was a biter." Kit squeezes his wrist like he can still feel it. "Anyway, one day they locked me in and never came back. I guess I fell asleep, and when social services stormed the place, none of those kids told them where I was. I was in there for three days before one of the kids finally cracked. But, ever since, I don't like the dark. And now, here we are," he says as he looks around. "Trapped in one big, giant trunk."

"I'm sorry." I swallow hard, trying to imagine what that must've been like. I feel like the biggest jerk, complaining about my family, when all they ever did was try to protect me.

Kit shrugs, but I can tell it still gets to him. "That's when I landed at Miss June's. She's sweet as molasses when the state comes around, but she's a stone-cold hustler. Taught me the ropes, though . . . how to cook her books . . . skim a little here and there. We have a mutual understanding. I stay out of her way and I get to keep the lights on. But sometimes, when we're kicking back on the front porch, watching the traffic on Eastridge Boulevard, it almost feels like we're a real family. It's better than being alone."

"I *love* being alone," Maria says. "I have my mommy and daddy, Nana, my two little sisters, and my auntie at my house. I can't even hear myself think sometimes."

"I like it over at your house," Darryl says. "At least your family talks. My dad works nights, Mom works days. There's never any music. No laughter." He tries to say it matter-of-fact, but I can hear the pain in his voice. "I come home from school, microwave a Lean Cuisine . . . I know what you're thinking . . . it's not really working. But the truth is I eat all kinds of junk when my mom goes to bed. We never talk about it, but she knows. She has to. I mean, she keeps buying it."

"Your diabetes!" Maria smacks him in the leg. "She knows you're not supposed to be eating that."

"What can I say? I have a sweet tooth, which is why I like you." He smiles down at her and Maria softens. "I watch *Judge Judy. Cops.* Maybe *Law and Order.* And then I fall asleep on the couch. They think it's because I'm too lazy to get up and move to my room," he says as he stares into the dark. "But I really just want them to *see* me. To remember that I exist. That way, they have no choice but to walk by their lump of a son."

"Don't talk about yourself like that," Maria says. "Words are weapons. The words we use to describe ourselves . . . they have power. We have to talk nice to ourselves. 'Cause most the time nobody else is going to."

As I'm listening to all of this, I'm thinking about my family, my friends, how they've never said an unkind word to me. Yeah, they didn't ask me about the incident, but they weren't the only ones burying what happened. There are a hundred times I could've spoken up and I didn't. I chose to live in that darkness because it was easier than fighting.

These people had the best excuses in the world to give up on life, but it didn't get in their way . . . it didn't stop them. They were fighting every day of their lives, and maybe there's still fight in me, too.

It's almost funny that it took getting trapped down here with a bunch of strangers to figure that out, but I feel a sliver of hope for the first time in a while. I'm not exactly sure what that entails, but it's the first time I can see an exit hatch—not the exit hatch I came down here for, but something else . . . something new.

I think about my friends up top, people I've known my entire life. I've never felt as close to any of them as I feel to Shy, Kit, Maria, and Darryl. Maybe it's just the stress of going through something like this, but I hope it's something more.

The thing is, we all have problems. Some have loving families, some have none. I'm rich and Kit's as poor as you can get. But we all want out—not just out of this cave but out of our circumstances. We all want to be better than we are.

But then I think about who I really am. What I've done.

A chill rushes over me.

Who am I kidding? They would never be friends with me if they knew the truth.

18

EVERYTHING'S completely still.

There's billowy pillows all around me.

A haze of tiny white particles dancing in the air.

I try to inhale, but my lungs won't let me. In a panic, I push away the pillows, bashing my knuckles against something—a steering wheel.

I'm in my car. And these are the air bags.

Fumbling with my seat belt, I grab my phone and open the door. A freezing burst of wind hits my face.

As I look back at the carnage, the air comes back to me in one violent gasp.

"Hey." Shy nudges me and I sit up like a shot, the heat bag crinkling all around me.

"Sorry, I must've fallen asleep. Here . . ." I start to get out of the bag. "Anyone need to warm up?" But no one seems to want it.

"Quickest way to warm up is to get moving," Shy says as she hands me the packet of beef Stroganoff. "The rest is for you."

I want to savor every cold, slimy bite, but everyone's waiting on me. I down it. My stomach groans with how good it feels, but it still can't fill the hole inside of me.

Darryl helps me to my feet. I've never felt an ache like this before. It's like I'm covered in one giant bruise.

"How long was I asleep?" I try to stretch out, but it only seems to make it worse.

"No clue. But you were talking."

"What?" I ask in alarm. "What did I say?"

"You kept saying, 'I don't remember anything.' It was kind of creepy, dude." Darryl helps me secure the pack on my shoulders. "You know that sound we heard before? We heard it again while you were out. If it's just our imagination, how come we're all hearing it, at the same time? Think about it," he says as he takes his place in the line.

I don't have an answer . . . for any of this.

I peer back into the darkness. If someone's down here, wouldn't they have spoken up by now? Made a move? Or maybe they haven't had the opportunity yet. To get me alone.

"Where's Grant?" Shy asks in annoyance.

"Coming," I say, turning my back on the darkness.

As we plod forward I'm thinking about all the things I took for granted. Food, shelter, fresh air. Sunlight is the big one. Without it I feel so . . . lost. Rudderless. No wonder those places up north have such a high suicide rate. Without light, what is there? It seems so basic, but I wonder if that's what happened to me these past few months. Maybe I just got so depressed I couldn't see the light anymore.

With Kit leading the way, joking around with Darryl and Maria, Shy lags behind. She's humming a tune I recognize, but I can't place it. Maybe a nursery rhyme, but it's prettier than that.

"What is that?" I ask. "The song."

She glances back at me over her shoulder, like she's embarrassed that I heard. "Mozart. Sonata in C Major."

"You know classical music?"

"Sure. Why wouldn't I?" She raises a brow. "You think only rich people listen to classical music?"

"No . . . that's not what I meant."

There's an awkward silence, but then she softens her tone. "My grandmother. She always wanted to play in an orchestra. The harp. But do you know how much a harp costs? It's ridiculous." She shakes her head. "Grandma Ruth sits in her favorite chair and plays the records. She closes her eyes. If you look close you can see her fingertips twitching along with the harp parts. She must've memorized them all."

I think about all the instruments that are collecting dust

in our house—pianos, flutes, violins—whatever Mare and I showed the slightest interest in.

"If we get out of here, I'm getting her a harp."

"I don't need your handouts."

"It's not for you. It's for your grandmother."

"You don't have to *buy* us anything." She peers back at me. "That's not how we choose our friends."

Her words hit me in the gut. I didn't think that's what I was doing, but maybe she's right. I've never had to make friends before. They were just kind of handed to me. "I didn't mean to make you feel uncomfortable . . . It's just, in my family, that's how we show we care about things."

She stops walking and lowers her voice. "Look, I don't need anything, but if you're serious about helping Kit . . . that would mean the world to me."

"Consider it done," I say as I hold out my pinky.

She looks down in amusement. "What are we, twelve?"

When I don't back down, she locks pinkies with me. "People say all kinds of things when they're in trouble, you know. When you get back to your posh life, you'll probably forget all about us."

"I'll never forget about this as long as I live. Especially you." I can't believe that just slipped out, but I'm not sorry.

Even though it's dark, I swear I can see her blush.

She pulls away and continues walking, but she didn't bite my head off, so I consider it a win.

"Just don't make promises you can't keep," she says under her breath.

Kit comes to an abrupt stop, and we all go crashing into one another. "Houston, we've got a problem."

Craning my neck, I try to see what the holdup is, but all I see is stone. Pushing forward through the tunnel, I come face-to-face with the rock wall. I run my hand over it, feeling a zigzag opening. It's so tight, even I'm nervous about getting through, but when I pull my hand back, there's a sticky substance clinging to my palm. "Guano," I whisper.

Shy looks up at me, a hint of a smile tugging on the corner of her mouth.

"Great. Another dead end." Darryl slumps against the wall.

"It's not a dead end. It's a squeeze." I try to keep my voice as calm and even as possible. "I read about this. Tough, but not impossible to get through."

Kit and Maria are small, so they'll be fine, and Shy is super athletic, so I think she'll be okay, but Darryl's another story.

Darryl makes his way forward, takes one look at the gap in the rock, and I can tell he's thinking the exact same thing.

"That's it. I'm screwed."

"Maybe we missed something." Maria says. "If we backtrack, we might be able to find another way—"

"We didn't miss anything," Shy says. "It's not like we sped by an exit on the highway. There's guano, which means this is where the bats went through."

"You guys are going to have to leave me," Darryl says.

Maria looks at Shy in a panic.

"We're not leaving anyone behind. I told you that," Shy assures them.

"Hey . . ." Kit holds up the flashlight to get everyone's attention. "Before we all start thinking about how we might have to chop up Darryl and eat him to survive, we need to see what we're dealing with." He slips inside the narrow crevice.

"Kit, wait." I start to go after him, but Shy holds me back.

"He's fine. He's used to getting out of tight spots."

I look down at her hand touching my arm, but she quickly pulls away.

"Guys," Darryl says with a nervous smile, "you wouldn't really eat me, right?"

"No. Of course not, baby." Maria hugs him, but I wonder if we would ever get to that point. The freeze-dried food isn't going to last forever.

There's a lot of straining noises coming from inside the squeeze, a loud thump, and then nothing.

"You all good?" Shy asks.

When he doesn't answer, we all gravitate toward the opening.

"Kit?" Maria calls out.

"Boo." He pokes his head through, scaring us half to death.

"Don't do that!" Shy yells as he climbs back through.

"It's not funny." Maria slaps his arm repeatedly.

"Okay . . . okay." Kit holds his hands in the air. "There's

a pretty big dip on the other side, but it looks like a clear path. This is the way out." Kit grins. "I can feel it."

Darryl lets out a burst of pent-up air. "But there's no way I'm going to fit in there. No way."

"You need to stay positive," Maria says.

"Um . . . I'm positive I'm too fat . . . How about that?"

"I told you not to talk like that. I don't like that."

"I'm not going to front," Kit says. "It's tight, but maybe we can push you through. Lube you up with something."

"That's your idea?" Maria knots her hands on her hips. "You want to oil him up and stuff him in . . . like a sausage?"

"It's not a bad idea." Darryl stands up a little taller. "Blubber can move . . . Look." He grabs his belly and gives it a hard shake.

"What do you think?" Shy looks at me.

"Yeah, it's worth a shot."

"Anything's better than being left behind," Darryl says.

"What can we use?" Shy asks.

I start digging through my pack, looking for anything that might work, but Kit's moved everything around. "Antibacterial gel?"

"That has alcohol in it," Maria says. "It's going to dry out his skin and burn if he gets scraped."

"There's this little packet of cortisone cream." I hold it up so she can inspect it, but she ignores me and starts rifling through her pockets.

"What is it?" Shy asks.

"Lip gloss," Maria says excitedly. "I have lip gloss." She pulls out the tube and hands it to me.

I check it out. "In your dreams."

"What's that supposed to mean?" Darryl asks.

"That's the name of the color." I take off the top and swipe it against the back of my hand. It's kind of a shimmery pink, but it seems slick enough. "This might work. Take off your shirt," I say as I step toward him.

"No way, dude."

I lower my voice. "I know it's uncomfortable, but you're going to have to–"

"No. It's not that. It's just . . . If anyone's rubbing me down with pink lip gloss, it's going to be my girl. No offense."

"Believe me . . ." I crack a smile as I hand it over to Maria. "None taken."

Darryl turns away from us to take off his shirt, and I can't help but feel sorry for him. I have to admit, I totally discounted him when I first saw him, but he's tough. I just want him to be comfortable in his own skin, because I don't see a big guy anymore, I just see Darryl. And he's really cool.

"Where should I put this?" Maria asks.

"Just focus on the midsection and the chest area," I say.

"You can call them man boobs," Darryl says. "Everyone else does."

"You're beautiful, just the way you are." Maria stands on her tiptoes to give him a quick kiss.

As Maria gets to work, I inspect the crevice. Using the file in my Swiss Army knife, I chisel down any of the sharp edges that might cut into him.

"All gone," Maria says, slipping the empty tube into her pocket.

I look back at him. The light from my headlamp falling over him makes him sparkle from the lip gloss.

Kit puts his hand over his mouth to stifle a laugh, but he can't hold it. "You look like the long-lost trailer park Cullen sibling."

"Ha. Ha. Very funny," Darryl replies. He wants to be mad, but as he looks down he starts cracking up. "I kind of do."

We're all laughing, desperate for some levity, but it quickly dies out.

As I'm getting everyone lined up, Darryl lifts his eyes to the ceiling. "Please let this work."

Kit goes through first, and then Shy. She has a little more trouble getting through than Kit, but once she arches her back, she slips right through. She's a natural at this. Probably a natural at everything.

"Maria, you should go next."

"No way, I'm staying with my Darryl."

I pull her aside. "He's going to need you on the other side. If he gets stuck, I'm going to need you to keep him calm. This could take awhile."

She nods and then takes Darryl's face in her hands. "You can do this. I'll be with you the entire time."

Darryl swallows so hard that I can hear it echo around us.

With one last look, Maria steps into the crevice. It takes her a couple of minutes to figure out how to twist her body along with the rock, but she makes it.

Darryl steps into position. He turns to me, anguish taking over his face. "Sorry you got stuck with this end."

"It's no big deal," I assure him. "Just helping out a friend, that's all."

"We *are* friends, aren't we?" he asks.

The sincerity—the vulnerability—catches me off guard. "Yeah . . . we are," I reply.

He gives me a crooked smile. "This must be what it's going to be like in the Marines. You should enlist with me. We'd have a blast."

"Maybe so." I place my hand on his shoulder, letting him know it's time.

"Here goes everything," he says as he releases a deep breath and leans into the crevice, pressing in as far as he can go.

A huge cheer resonates from the other side. "We can see his head!"

He calls back, "Don't they say if you get your head through, the rest will follow?"

I'm pretty sure that only applies to rodents, but I don't want to discourage him. "Yeah. You're doing great." I place my hand on his stomach to help him get in a good position, and he flinches.

"It's okay. Just think of what I'm doing like a really intense massage."

"A massage? Like I've ever had a massage. You're funny, Grant."

Darryl's skin is ice cold. If he goes into shock, I wonder how long it would take for hypothermia to set in down here?

"Shy?" I call through the slit. "What should he do next?"

"He needs to twist his torso and get his left arm through. That will give him more leverage."

"Okay, Darryl. You heard her."

As he exhales, he twists his torso to the right, so he can make room for his left arm to squeeze forward. I help him, pushing his meaty shoulder through the gap. He's grunting with the strain, and when he gets his arm through the gap, everyone starts cheering again.

"I did it." He pants.

"Now what, Shy?"

"He needs to arch his back and push against the rock with both arms to pull himself through."

"Piece of cake." Darryl tries to laugh, but he can't. He's in there too tight. I really hope he doesn't break any ribs.

"Let me know when you're ready," I tell him. "Same thing. Exhale, and then push with everything you've got."

As soon as he gets control of his breath, he exhales and starts fighting—against the rock, against himself, against death.

I put all my weight behind him. I hear his skin scraping against the rock, but I can't stop, I can't let up. I can't give up on him. With every inch won, the notion of us getting through this, surviving this cave, grows in me. And I can't help thinking that if I can somehow save them, I might be able to save myself. With one last burst of strength, I push until I feel his body give way.

I hear a loud thump, followed by a joyous burst of nervous laughter.

"He's clear," Maria cries.

"Sorry for using up all your lip gloss," Darryl says. "I know that was your favorite."

"You're my favorite," Maria replies. I can hear her kiss him.

"Get a room," Shy says.

"All right, V, you're up," Kit calls through the gap.

"V?" I ask.

"Isn't that part of your name? The Roman numeral for five?"

"Yeah. I've just never had a nickname before."

"Well, that's just sad. Now you do."

It's funny that something so simple like that can make me smile, especially in a place like this.

As I'm shoving my pack through, I hear something behind me. That wordless whisper, like someone's on the verge of telling me the answer to everything. My heart's pounding as I step toward the darkness, but there's nothing there. I know this is probably my imagination, the dark getting to me, but it feels so real.

"What do you want?" I whisper, only to hear my words

reverberate back to me. Something about it creeps me out even more. All I know is if there's something down here, and if it's as big as it seems, there's no way it's getting through that squeeze.

It takes everything I have to turn my back on it, but I can't give in to the fear. I have people counting on me.

Easing into the crevice, I start working my body through, cocking my head, arching my back, trying to push my chest forward, but something's not quite working. Instead of trying to force it, I stop and take a breath. There's a certain rhythm to getting through a squeeze. I just have to find it.

I try to relax into it, breathe into the stone.

Inhale, gather strength.

Exhale, push.

I manage to get half of my left arm through, up to my elbow, before I'm stopped.

"Hey, you all right in there?" Shy asks.

I feel an embarrassed flush take over my face. I'm the one who's supposed to be an expert at all this. So much for me trying to impress her. "I must've gone in at a bad angle. Let me back up and try again."

But as I try to pull back, I soon realize I'm stuck. Dead stuck.

I let out a shaky breath.

"Everything okay, V?" Kit asks.

I try to shake it off, and go at it again, but I can't budge.

"I don't understand. I thought I did exactly what you

guys did." I grunt as I try to back out again. "I must've hit it wrong."

Shy shines the light in the crevice, trying to see what the problem is.

She pulls.

I push.

With sweat running down my face, my breath shallow and weak, I do everything I can think of to pry myself loose, either way, but there's no give. I only seem to be wedging myself in deeper.

I try to wet my lips but I only end up licking stone. The taste of wet earth fills my mouth, my throat, spreading through my body like an infection, until I feel like I've become one with the cave. That maybe I belong here. That I died a long time ago.

> *"Darkling I listen; and, for many a time*
> *I have been half in love with easeful Death,*
> *Call'd him soft name in many a musèd rhyme,*
> *To take into the air my quiet breath,"* I whisper.

I'm not sure how much time passes in this state, but it feels like days. I might have even blacked out for a while, because the next thing I know, Shy's slapping my cheeks.

"Stay with me, Grant Franklin Tavish the fifth. Do you hear me? It's time to wake up. We're not letting you go. You have work to do."

I focus in on her soft brown eyes, the hollows of her

cheekbones, the determined shape of her mouth, and all I can think is she's the most beautiful thing I've ever seen. Like an angel.

A wave of sound rushes through the tunnel up ahead. For a moment, I think it's another collapse, but the stone isn't trembling. The sound's growing stronger and stronger by the second. Shy, Kit, Maria, and Darryl all turn, shining their flashlights toward the thundering din as a flood of bats sweeps through a connecting tunnel up ahead.

"Go," I yell as forcefully as I can. "Follow them. That's the way out. You have the supplies you need. I want you to go."

But, instead, they switch off the flashlights again, even Kit.

"We're not going anywhere," Shy says, and they all gather around the opening, putting their hands on me. "We're in this together."

The gesture fills me with so much emotion I can hardly stand it—guilt, hope, fear. Tears are streaming down my face and I know this is a pivotal moment for me. If I don't make it out of this squeeze, I'll die down here. And, for the first time since the incident, I don't want that to happen. I want to live.

"My shoulder," I pant. "If you can pull it out of the socket, it might give me the inch I need to get through."

"You want us to break your arm?" Shy asks.

"Just dislocate it. It's happened before, playing lacrosse, so it should come out fairly easy. Maria . . . Maria can do it."

Shy pulls her forward.

"He's not thinking straight." Maria peeks her head in the crevice. "I've only seen someone reset an arm before, and I've definitely never seen anyone pull one out on purpose."

"First time for everything." I smile up at her wearily.

"I can't believe I'm doing this." Maria reaches in, prying her hand in as deep as she can get, gripping my elbow. She looks scared. "You know, this is going to hurt. And if I don't do this right, I could tear all the ligaments and you won't be able to—"

"Please."

"Okay . . ." She licks her lips and looks back at Shy, who gives her a reassuring nod.

I grit my teeth, my breath coming out in short bursts through my nose, like a bull. The waiting for it, the anticipation—that seems to be the hardest part.

"I can't do it." She draws back.

"If you don't do it, I'm going to die down here. Is that what you want?" I don't mean to scream at her, but I'm at the end of my rope.

Without saying another word, Maria digs in, gives my arm a hard yank and then a twist.

I let out an agonized scream, but it's exactly the give I need to get through. They pull me out and I fall to the ground, bashing my arm against the cold stone floor.

Maybe it's the pain or the cold or the exhaustion, but it feels like this cave just gave birth to me. That I've somehow been given a second chance. How many chances can one person get? How many chances do I deserve?

Writhing on the floor, I'm relieved to be on the other side, but I know it's not over yet.

"Hold him still," Maria says as she crouches next to me.

I clench my eyes shut, trying to think of anything pleasant—Christmas morning, skiing down fresh powder on a black diamond, catching the perfect wave—but my mind wanders back to Shy. I hardly know her, but there's something about her that makes me want to be a better person. The type of man who does the right thing.

"I'm going to pop it back in," Maria says as she gets behind me, a firm grip on my elbow and my shoulder.

The pain's gnawing away at my senses; my nerves are firing. The anticipation feels like waiting for an ax to fall.

"On the count of three. One. Two. Three—"

Maria heaves my arm up and in, forcing it back into the socket.

As I collapse on the ground, rocking back and forth, trying not to pass out, I know I have to tell Shy the truth. I have to tell all of them.

They deserve to know what kind of person they're risking their lives for.

19

THE shock and adrenaline keep me going for a while, but I can feel my body shutting down. I look at Darryl, thinking he must be just as tired as I am, but he seems to be holding up. I still can't believe he was able to get through easier than me. I'm just glad we all made it.

As soon as we reach a fairly dry spot, I clear my throat. "I think I need to rest for a while."

Shy gives a nod and everyone stops.

She was right. I need to start saying how I feel. Being honest with myself and others. I'll be no use to anyone if I fall and break my leg down here.

As we settle in a circle, Kit takes out the heat bag and they help me get in. I don't even argue. I must have a fever, because my teeth are chattering so hard, I'm afraid they'll break. Darryl gathers Maria in his arms, and Shy and Kit sit on either side of me.

"All we need is a fire," Darryl says as he pretends to warm his hands over a campfire, rubbing them together briskly. "And s'mores."

"Hey, we have ice cream." Kit perks up, digging through the bag. "We should celebrate."

"Celebrate?" I ask.

"We saw the bats, which means we're on the right track. I mean, yeah, it's the only track, but whatever. I think we're really close to getting out of here."

Kit divides the square and passes the pieces around.

Maybe it's just the sugar going straight to their brains, but they seem happy. Giddy almost. It's hard not to get caught up in it, but when I think about the bats, I think about getting to the surface. And when that happens, they're going to learn all about me. I can't let them find out that way. I have to come clean about who I really am. What I did. Why I came down here in the first place. Maybe they'll take the supplies and leave . . . decide I don't deserve to make it out of here.

I have to take that chance.

Kit hands me a chunk of the ice cream that I suspect is a much bigger piece than anyone else got, but I shake my head.

"I'll save yours for later," he says as he puts it back in the package.

I can tell they're all worried about me. And it almost

makes it worse. The way they trusted me. Welcomed me. Saved me.

"How long do you think we've been down here?" Kit asks. "We should start a pool."

"Gambling goes against your probation," Shy says.

"Who's going to tell?"

"Well, according to Darryl, we're being monitored down here by the military . . . or aliens." She starts laughing.

"Shut up, Shy." Darryl tries not to smile. "Just watch. If it ends up being true, you're going to be sorry."

"I'm already sorry." Shy pulls her knees into her chest, resting her chin on top. "I really hope we make it back in time for my trials on Monday. A bunch of scouts are going to be there from colleges . . . the Olympic committee. I've got a lot riding on this."

"Yeah, I know what you mean," Darryl says. "I have an appointment at the recruitment center for my physical. Third time's the charm. And Maria's supposed to go down to VCCS this week."

"Fingers crossed on that financial aid package," she says.

"This is going to sound pathetic." Kit leans back. "But I'm just looking forward to taco night." Everyone starts cracking up. "I'm serious. Miss June goes all out. Sour cream and everything," he says with that easy grin.

"How about you, V?"

I look at them, every single one of them, and I know this is it. My chance to come clean. "Court." I swallow hard. "I have a court appearance on Monday."

"Why?" Shy asks, her back stiffening.

It takes everything I have to keep going, but I have to do this. I don't know where to start . . . so I just start from the beginning.

"Christmas break. I went to Lewis Banner's party. His parents had already left for Greenbrier. It was out of control, as usual. A lot of drinking, weed, just blowing off steam. I mean, it's our last year of high school. And, according to our parents, the best time of our lives. I went looking for Lewis. I just wanted to tell him some people from Trinity were breaking into his parents' wine cellar. I went upstairs, found him in his room . . . with Catherine." I bite down on the inside of my cheek. "My girlfriend at the time."

"Ooh, that's gotta hurt." Darryl scrunches up his face.

"Maybe they were just talking," Maria says.

"Trust me. They weren't talking."

"Trifling." Kit shakes his head.

"Did you hit the guy?" Darryl asks.

"That's the thing . . ." I try to swallow, but it feels like my throat is caked with dust. "I just stood there. I didn't know what to do. I stormed out, got in my car—if you could call that thing a car. Range Rover, with all the best safety features money can buy. More like a tank." My eyes dart around the circle, but I can't look them directly in the eyes. "I was buzzed, but I was fine to drive. At least I thought I was fine. I mean, I'd done it a bunch of times before. We all had."

"Did you get pulled over?" Maria asks.

"I wish." I stare at the imaginary fire between us. "I wish that happened. I don't know what I was thinking. I just needed a little space." I rock forward, trying to find my breath. "The thing is, yeah, I was embarrassed, but after I got about a mile away, I felt more relieved than anything else. I didn't really feel angry. I guess I just needed to *seem* mad . . . to save face. Which says a lot about my life, how numb I was to everything."

"How long were you dating her?" Shy asks.

"Years." I meet her gaze. "Ever since she asked me to Freshman Fling. It was always expected in a way."

"What . . . like an arranged marriage?"

"I guess." I give a halfhearted shrug. "The Tavish and Gray families have a long history."

"So what happened when you went back to the party?" Maria asks.

"I never made it back." I let out a shivering breath. "It had just started to snow. It wasn't cold enough to stick, but it made everything glimmer in the moonlight. I saw headlights up ahead . . . but they didn't see me. I guess I forgot to put mine on. They had this old Buick. No air bags. Some of them weren't even wearing seat belts. Just one inch over the line. One inch. That's all it was." I close my eyes for a moment so I can get this out. "I smashed into their left headlight and they went spinning. Flipped over. My air bags exploded on all sides. I couldn't see. I couldn't breathe. But I could hear it. Screeching tires, crushing metal, screams . . . and then nothing. But it wasn't nothing." I blink back tears.

"I remember grabbing my phone, getting out of the car. The snow falling gently all around me, sticking to my eyelashes. I remember the sound of my footsteps. The dull pulsing light from one of their taillights. The smell of hot oil sizzling as it dripped onto the icy pavement. A whisper. And the next thing I knew, my father's lawyer was leading me back to the car, buckling me back in, giving me charcoal tablets, telling me *You don't remember anything.* When I glanced up at him, I didn't even recognize him. He looked like one of those soldiers stumbling out of the front lines from an old war movie. The sheer horror on his face. This is someone I've known my whole life. And he looked at me like I was a monster.

"The ambulance didn't even put on the sirens. They just took them away in bags. Like meat." The back of my throat burns at the memory.

"It's strange . . . you look at a pole, a DEER CROSSING sign, a gearshift, a windshield . . . they're just objects. But when you hit something with that much force, everything becomes a weapon." I wipe my sweaty palms against my pants.

"They should've taken me away in cuffs. Charged me with something . . . anything." I raise my head. "But I'm the son of Senator Grant Tavish the fourth. And things like that don't happen to Tavishes. By the time I got to the hospital to get checked out, my lawyer had already negotiated the terms behind closed doors. Three months' suspended license and weekly drug tests. Barely a slap on the wrist. I got away with murder." I clench my jaw. "It's ironic that in order to avoid hurting Lewis, giving him a quick pop in the jaw, I went out and killed a carful of people."

"Is that why you think someone followed you down here?" Shy asks. "For revenge?"

I nod. "There were death threats, news stories with 'affluenza' all over them. A couple of strange things happened, but it was more of a feeling. My parents did their best to protect me. No internet, no one was allowed to speak of the incident in front of me. All I had to do was show up for court on Monday and say those four words— *I don't remember anything*—and all of this would be taken care of. Erased."

I shake my head. "But as hard as they tried to make me forget, all I could do was remember." I glance up toward the ceiling. "Little bits and pieces came filtering in. I remember everything up until I was standing in front of the other car. I still don't understand how the lawyer got there before the police. But maybe I just don't want to remember. Maybe I've buried it so deep that I never will." I pull the recovery bag tighter around me. "Betray my family or betray myself. Those were my choices. But I had something else in mind." I swallow back the bile threatening to come up.

"I planned it for months, every little detail, to make it look like an accident. But when the collapse happened—"

"That's why you had the knife in your hand?" Shy says.

I look up at her, at all of them, which makes it hurt even worse. "I was so close to cutting that rope," I whisper.

Shy leans forward. "What made you change your mind?"

"I saw you." I take in a trembling breath. "I didn't want you to die because of me . . . because of my mistakes. But more than that . . . I know it's time to face this."

Shy slips her hand into mine. Her fingers are ice cold, but I don't flinch. I don't dare to move.

No one says *Don't worry . . . It's not your fault . . . It could've been any one of us.*

It's not forgiveness but acknowledgment that this actually happened. And that's all I ever wanted.

Tears sting my eyes as I close my hand around hers and hold on tight—tighter than I've ever held on to anything in my entire life. Here in the dark, it feels like she's the only thing keeping me grounded. Keeping me sane.

20

I WAKE up in pure darkness. It's so dark that I can't even tell if my eyes are open or shut. I have to put my finger in my eye so I can tell. Which sounds crazy, but this kind of dark, this kind of nothingness, does things to you. I don't know how long we've been asleep; it's impossible to keep track of time down here. I counted two hundred and sixteen drips before I dozed off. I think I dreamed, but of what, I'm not sure. It felt like I had nightmares, but what could possibly be more bleak than this?

Kit's batteries must've burned out again. I want to switch them out before he wakes up, but when I turn on my headlamp I notice that Shy is still holding my hand.

I don't want to move; I'm afraid she might wake up, come to her senses, and let go.

I've been trying not to look at her too much, but she really is stunning. Especially in the dim light, the shadows sinking into the hollows of her cheekbones. She has this tense, determined look on her face when she's awake, but here, in sleep, she's completely relaxed . . . vulnerable. Her mouth is soft; her eyelashes are long and dark. I want to run my thumb over that little spot between her eyes that's always furrowed up, but that would be way too creepy under even the most normal of circumstances.

When her eyes flutter open, I quickly look away, but I'm pretty sure she caught me.

I turn my attention to Kit's flashlight, but it's nowhere to be found. Neither is Kit.

Shy notices my gaze and sits up. "Kit?" she calls out as she tries to smooth down her hair.

Maria and Darryl stir awake.

"He's probably just taking a leak," Darryl says as he squints down the tunnel.

"Kit? You there?" Maria calls out.

"Dude." Darryl sighs. "If you're messing with us, you can cut it out. Not the time or the place."

I put my hand down on the damp stone to push myself up, and when I go to grab my pack, I see that my palm is streaked with red. At first I think it's just a trick of the light, but then Maria peers over my shoulder. "Are you bleeding?"

"I don't think so," I say as she inspects my hand. But

when I point the light toward the ground, we see a trail of deep red leading down the dark tunnel.

"I swear to God, Kit . . ." Shy squares herself in front of the tunnel. "If this is another one of your jokes, I'm going to kill you."

As we move forward in one huddled mass, following the trail, the cave feels a little colder . . . a little darker.

"Maybe he got a bloody nose," Maria says.

But when the deep red drops turn into one long, continuous swath, I know it's something more than that. It looks like either he dragged himself down the cave . . . or something dragged him.

The trail opens up to a cathedral-size cavern covered in long, calcified spikes shooting up from the floor in every direction, like hundreds of jagged teeth.

I'm panning my headlamp over the strange formations when Shy grabs my chin with her trembling hand, steering the light back toward the left, illuminating a pair of dead eyes.

Immediately, I start dry heaving, my gut reacting before I can even register what I'm seeing.

Darryl staggers back; Maria holds on to him.

But Shy just stands there, like a statue, that same hollow look on her face. It makes me wonder what she's seen in her life.

Using all my strength, I force myself to look up. There, suspended in midair, facing the ceiling, Kit is splayed out, a stalagmite protruding from his chest as if he's been skewered like a piece of meat.

"This can't be real," Darryl says as he grabs his skull. "We're still asleep, right?"

As much as I want to pretend it's all in our heads, I can smell death in the air. I know that smell.

"Kit," Shy whispers, her breath shallow in her chest. "How could this have happened?"

I'm searching the cavern, my brain, for any kind of clue, but my head is spinning. "There has to be a logical explanation," I manage to get out.

"Give me one logical explanation," Maria says, a sharp edge to her voice.

"We all felt something . . . We all heard the noises," Darryl says. "What if there really is someone down here with us? Stalking us?"

"If that's true, it's *him* they're after. Not us." Maria begins to pace. "Or maybe *he's* the one who did this," she says, backing away from me. "Think about it . . . We know he's a killer. Maybe he felt bad about his little confession and now he wants us dead before we can tell anyone. Maybe we're next."

I open my mouth to tell her I would never hurt Kit or any one of them, but nothing comes out. I can't even breathe. Is that what she really thinks of me . . . what they all think of me?

Darryl grabs onto Maria, pulling her in for a hug. "You didn't mean that. Grant's our friend. He would never do anything like that."

"*Kit* was our friend." Maria's shoulders begin to shake.

Darryl shoots me a look of apology, but I can't bear to meet his eyes.

"The worst thing we can do down here is panic and start turning on each other," Shy says in a low, measured voice, but she never takes her eyes off Kit's body.

"He probably stumbled in here to take a leak and got confused," Darryl says. "Maybe he tripped."

"Tripped backwards onto one of these spears?" Maria pulls away from him, her anger flaring back up. "There's no way that could've happened if he just stumbled back." She kicks one of the stalagmites, sending it crashing to the floor. It sounds like bones being shattered. "There was force . . . It's like someone picked him up off the ground and dropped him."

I shine my headlamp up the side of the cavern, to the towering ceiling–

There's a flash of movement. Whatever it is . . . it's big.

Feeling the blood drain from my face, I stagger back, but the form moves with me. I brace my hand in front of Shy to protect her, when I realize it's only my shadow. "Jesus." I let out a heavy breath.

"Could he have tried to climb?" Darryl asks.

"I'm going to find out." Gripping onto a slick jag of rock, I start to ascend, but Shy pulls me back.

"We can't risk something happening to you, too."

I stare up at the ceiling. "If he got high enough, lost his grip and fell back . . . It's possible . . . The velocity could've driven the stalagmite right through him."

"Why?" Maria wipes the tears from her face with the back of her hand. "Why would he do that?"

"To get out," Shy says. "Who knows what he thought he saw up there . . . or what he thought he was running from. The dark . . . the rapture . . . maybe it got to him." She looks up at me, and I can see how scared and heartbroken she is, but she's desperately trying to hold it together . . . for all of us. "Whatever happened, this was an accident. A tragic accident," she says. "Nothing more."

"What do we do?" I ask, staring back at Kit's body.

Shy takes a deep breath. "We have to keep going."

"Okay," I say as I start digging through my pack. "We can use the heat bag to make a stretcher and—"

"No." She shakes her head. "We have to leave him."

"We can't," I argue, my blood running cold at the prospect. "We can't leave him like that," I say as I approach his body, trying to figure out how to get him down. "At the very least we have to—"

"Don't touch him." Maria steps in front of me. "The police will need to see how he died. Make sure there wasn't foul play."

"And dude, there's no way we can carry someone out of here." Darryl's shoulders slump. "We don't even know if we can get ourselves out of here."

"But Kit—"

"This isn't Kit anymore," Shy says, her dark eyes piercing through the dim light. "Kit was full of life. The best thing we can do for him is remember him . . . the way he was. The way he wanted to be."

As I take a step back, I accidentally kick something with my boot. It's a flashlight. *Property of Kit Jackson.* I turn it on. A fresh wave of pain washes over me when I see it come to life.

"He didn't like the dark," I whisper as I gently place it on his chest, the light creating a soft halo around him.

I know it's a waste of resources, but no one argues about it. Not even Maria.

As we walk away from the cavern, deeper into the belly of this living tomb, I watch the glow from Kit's flashlight grow dimmer and dimmer.

In the beginning, I thought of this cave as a benevolent presence, one that meant us no harm, but the more time I spend down here, the more I'm beginning to fear that I had it all wrong.

Maybe this cave doesn't want us to get out of here alive.

21

FOR the longest time, we don't say anything.

What can we possibly say?

Our friend just died in the most horrific way possible and we have no idea how it happened . . . how he felt in the end . . . what was going through his mind.

I've taken the lead since we found Kit. They say it's because I have the best light, but I know it's because they don't completely trust me. And maybe they shouldn't. I'm the only outsider here. I wouldn't be surprised if I looked back to find them gone. I wouldn't blame them a bit if they decided to bail. Maria's right. If there is someone down here, it's me they're after. Not them.

I look down at my hands, wondering if I could've had

anything to do with Kit's death. There's no blood beneath my nails, no sign of a struggle, but my hands seem to be opening and closing slower now. Maybe it's all in my head, or hypothermia setting in. All I know is that we're starting to unravel.

During our breaks, we turn off all the lights. Mostly it's to conserve batteries, but I think the main reason is we just can't look at each other anymore. Not after what happened. Darryl's spending more time talking to himself, or the walls, than he's talking to the others. Every time Maria looks at me I wonder if she's going to hack me into a million pieces. And Shy's quiet. At times, she gets so still that I wonder if she's even breathing.

Sometimes I think I can hear Kit laughing—or not really laughing, but the smile in his voice. It's hard to believe we were just talking about all the things we wanted to do when we get out of here . . . but maybe that was a long time ago. It's impossible to get a grip on time when there's only darkness.

I'm straining to remember anything that might help us get out of here, but my brain feels like it's submerged under heavy water. And once you stop remembering, once you block out the past, there's no hope of a future. I know that too well. If I let myself slip back into that numbness, I'm doomed.

Forcing my thoughts to go back to that night, I remember the responding officer's face. I remember every line, every freckle, his icy blue eyes trying to stare the truth out of me. How can I remember that and not remember what happened after I got out of the car? How did my lawyer get there first? The memory feels so close, like it's right in front of me, but I can't find it.

"It's time," Shy whispers.

I reach out for her, but she's already stepped away from me.

Turning on my headlamp, I'm relieved to still find them with me. They turn on the remaining two flashlights in response.

As we move forward, into a narrow shaft, I have the strangest feeling—the dark pressing in all around me, it feels thicker than air. I don't know if it's the humidity or something more, but every step seems to be harder than the last. Maybe it's dread.

A low growl reverberates through the cave. At first, I think it's Darryl's stomach, but when I feel the growl travel right under my feet, I know it's something much deeper than that. Whatever it is, I know we all felt it, because we're standing there staring at one another, afraid to name it, afraid to acknowledge that something very bad is about to happen.

When the grumble passes through again, it's followed by a sharp cracking sound, like a million chestnuts popping in a fire. I follow the hairline fracture with my light, watching it worm its way down the tunnel, right under our feet, and I know exactly what's coming.

Collapse. I try to get the word out, but my breath hitches in my throat.

Grabbing Shy's hand, I pull her forward. We're running through the tunnel, there's screaming, breaking rock, and then a huge explosion as the passageway starts collapsing beneath us. Spotting a connecting tunnel on the left, I pull Shy inside. She yanks Maria with her, but as the dust settles we realize, Darryl's nowhere to be found.

Shy's hugging Maria, trying to console her, when Darryl coughs out, "Help."

"Darryl," Maria screams as she tries to get to him, but Shy holds her back.

I peer over the edge to find him dangling there, nothing but the cold, black deep beneath him.

"Brace me," I call back to Shy as I get flat on the ground.

With Maria and Shy hanging on to my legs, I reach down for Darryl, but he's only focused on the depths below.

"I'm here, Darryl. Grab on," I tell him, but he doesn't answer, doesn't even look at me. "There's something wrong with him," I call back.

"Heights," Maria says. "He's deathly afraid of heights."

I remember him peeking over the ledge and then backing up against the tunnel when they first found me.

Grasping his forearms, I try to pull him up, but he's fighting me. "Just let go and we'll do the rest."

"I can't," he whispers. "Get Maria to the surface, that's all I ask."

I feel my body slowly slipping forward, my muscles screaming for rest. I hate having to play this card, but I'm desperate. "You know Maria will never leave you. If you don't grab onto me, you're not only signing your death sentence but you'll be signing hers, as well."

He looks up at me in anguish. "No."

"Our only chance of surviving this is if we stick together. All of us. We owe that to Kit."

His bottom lip trembles.

An ill wind moves through the cave and I watch a visible chill wash over him.

"All you have to do is grab onto me. One hand at a time. But whatever you do . . . don't look down."

He nods rapidly, his eyes watering up. "Don't look down . . . Don't look down." He repeats it like a mantra.

"Which arm do you want to do first?"

"Left."

"My left or your left?"

"I don't know," he yells, his fingers turning purple from the strain. "You're confusing me."

"Nod toward the arm you want to let go of first." He nods toward his left. "Got it." I squeeze his wrist.

He's about to let go, when a scattering of rocks comes from below.

"Did you hear that?" he says, staring down into the abyss.

"It's nothing. Just the rock settling. That happens. We're almost there."

But he keeps looking down, whispering.

"What are you trying to say?" I lean over as far as possible so I can get more leverage. "I can't hear you."

Darryl's breathing so hard I'm afraid he's going to pass out, but maybe that would be the best option at this point. Then we could just pull him up without a fight.

"Grant, you need to come back," Shy yells. "You're slipping. I don't know how much longer we can hold you."

"Don't you dare give up on him," Maria screams. "Baby, you need to get up here right now. Do you hear me? I need you."

That seems to get his attention for a moment, but then we hear another scattering of rocks. This time closer.

"You heard that, right?" His voice cracks.

Before I can even answer, we hear it again.

Even closer.

"There's something down here," Darryl whispers. "A monster. I know you feel it, too."

"All we have to do is get you to solid ground," I say as I try to coax him along. "And then we can talk about it all you want."

As Darryl's fingertips finally slip off the ledge, he grabs onto me, but he's panicking like he's in a free fall, screaming at the top of his lungs, "Something touched me . . . Something grabbed my foot. We're all going to die down here." And then he starts pulling himself up my body. If I don't calm him down, he could yank us both right off the ledge.

"Darryl!" I try to look him straight in the eyes, to tell him everything's going to be okay, when he grabs my headlamp, ripping it off my head.

He climbs up the rest of my body, not caring if he rips

me off the ledge in the process, and I watch the light sail to the bottom of the chasm, sinking like a stone between two enormous boulders. My heart sinks with it.

As Shy and Maria pull me up to safety, there's no joyous cheer, no collective sigh of relief.

This is a harsh reality check.

Slumped against the side of the tunnel, I pull off my pack and start going through the supplies. I've always been able to find a certain amount of comfort in taking inventory, organizing things, but it doesn't work this time. "We're down to one flashlight, a box of matches, and a single candle."

I try not to let it show, but I can tell by the way Shy is looking at me that she gets it. If we don't find our way to the surface soon, we'll run out of light. And without light, our lives will slowly be extinguished.

As if Darryl realizes the gravity of what he's done, he curls up in a ball and begins to cry. "I'm sorry. I'm so sorry, dude. I don't know what happened to me."

"You panicked, that's all," Maria says as she rubs his back. She looks up at me and I know what she wants from me.

"We're all good," I tell him, pulling out the last bag of food as a peace offering.

He sits up, wiping the tears from his red, swollen eyes, and takes the packet.

We sit in silence, staring into the dark tunnel before us, each taking turns with the macaroni and cheese. I should be starving, but I can hardly get it down.

My body feels like one of those cold, slippery noodles. All I want to do is lie down and rest, but I'm afraid I'll never get back up again.

"We need to keep moving." I struggle to pull myself up, swaying a little as I put the pack on my shoulders. Shy steadies me.

"But we need to talk about what happened," Darryl says as he follows after me.

"You panicked. We lost a light. It happens. The important thing is that you're okay."

"No. Not that. The thing . . . the thing that grabbed me."

"I told you." I keep my head down, focusing on the ground in front of me. "This is what the dark does to people. You need to shake it off."

"Shake it off?" He grabs my shoulder, stopping me. "I know what I felt . . . and you heard it. I know you did. The whisper."

I look up at him sharply, my stomach tightening into a hard knot. "What difference would it make? Would it change anything? We're still trapped down here with basically nothing to defend ourselves with. All we can do is keep going."

"Listen to him," Maria says soothingly. "I didn't see anything. Shy didn't see anything. And we were there the entire time. We need to stick together, now more than ever." She brushes her hand over his back and I see an ease pass over him.

"Maybe you're right." He nods his head a little too

rapidly, like he's trying to convince himself, more than anything. "Yeah. It could be all in my head. Like special ops training," he reasons. "When they try to break you down with sensory deprivation but you know it's not real."

"Exactly." Maria exhales. "You're stronger than that."

"Yeah . . . yeah . . . that makes sense," he mutters to himself.

As Maria and Darryl lag behind, it gives me a chance to check on Shy. I can tell she doesn't want to talk about it, but when she reaches out to hold my hand, I know that she's okay. That *we're* okay. Even down here, there's still something good to be found.

As the path opens up into a wide Y formation, we fan out.

There's a tunnel to the left and a tunnel to the right.

"It's the Keyhole Passage," I say, looking around in wonder. "I remember this from the guidebook. It's part of the old system. The south exit isn't far from here."

"Are you serious?" Shy asks breathlessly. "Which way?"

I hold my head in my hands, like I can squeeze the memory to the surface, but I'd only be guessing. "I . . . I can't remember, but one of the sides is a dead end."

"Wait . . . I know how to do this." Darryl steps forward. "I know how to find the right way."

"How?" Shy asks.

"From *Doom*," Darryl says, his confidence returning.

Maria's eyes go wide. "That stupid video game?"

"It's not stupid. It's super realistic. I just need the matches."

I'm hesitant to hand them over, but I can tell he's just trying to make amends, trying to be helpful. And I know what a second chance can mean to a person.

Digging out the box from my pack, I hand them over.

"Watch the flame," he says as he goes about twenty feet into the first tunnel and turns around to face us. Striking a match, he holds it up, and we watch the flame flicker gently toward his face. "See? There's air moving through here. Now, let's check to see if it's stronger on this side," he says as he goes into the other tunnel. He turns to face us and strikes the match, which promptly burns out.

"Sorry. That must've been a dud."

As Maria's rubbing her arms, trying to get warm, Darryl strikes another one. Same thing happens.

"That's weird," he says.

"Is the air blowing it out?" she asks.

"No. That's the thing. It feels dead still in here, but it's like something's blowing it out . . . maybe from above."

As he strikes another match, he looks up.

The color leaches from his face.

A wet spot blooms at his crotch.

"Grant—" he manages to call out before the match goes out.

Before I can even think of responding, Darryl's body is jerked straight into the air, slammed against the cave ceiling, and then dropped back to the ground with a dense thud.

22

AS we rush in, Maria skids to the ground and gathers Darryl in her arms. I try to chase after the hulking shadow, but I quickly lose track. Whatever it is, it's using the darkness as a shield. I take another step forward and I swear I can feel the dark penetrating my skin, seeping into every hollow space inside of me, wanting to consume me.

The matchbox is on the ground. When I bend over to pick it up, I hear the whisper, luring me forward.

"Grant." Shy's voice pulls me back. "I need you."

Running back, I find Darryl lying limp in Maria's arms like a rag doll. Half of his head is caved in, but she doesn't seem to notice.

Shy and I stand there, watching in horror, as she tries

to revive him. As the air inflates his chest, I see his fingertips flicker, but I know it's only a random impulse. I've seen it before. He's gone. Death on impact. The light has left his eyes, but Maria refuses to accept it.

"Time to wake up now," she says as she smooths her hand over his bashed-in face.

Shy squeezes Maria's shoulder. "He's gone," she says softly.

"No he's not." Maria jerks away from her touch. "He's just tired, that's all. He's always been a heavy sleeper."

"Maria, look at me." Shy tightens her grip and shakes her. "He's dead."

Maria holds her breath. I hold mine, too. It's like we're all just waiting for someone to wake us up from this nightmare, but it never happens.

Shy's words seem to slowly sink in, because Maria bursts into tears and then screams into the tunnel, "What kind of monster would do this?"

The sound that answers back would be horrifying to most people, but to us it's like a dream: the screeching echo of hundreds of wings flapping in the tunnel next to us.

"We have to go," Shy says as she pulls at her. "We have to follow them."

Maria blinks, but I can tell she's not entirely grasping what's happening.

"Help me," Shy says to me.

We lift Maria to her feet, forcing her to let go of Darryl's hand. It's one of the most painful things I've ever had to do.

As we're dragging her down the other tunnel, I can see

it in her eyes: on some level, Maria still blames me for this. I would've gladly taken Darryl's place—Kit's as well—but that's not what happened. The only thing I can do is make sure she gets out of here alive.

We follow the sound of the bats as long as we can, but Maria is starting to fall more than she can get back up. We're beyond exhausted. Beyond feeling human.

When we reach a deep recess in the cave wall, I motion for them to step inside. Shy pulls Maria into the crevice as far as they can go, and I duck in after them. The walls of the recess are completely smooth, like it's been carved out with an ice-cream scoop. It's a good hiding spot, where nothing will be able to sneak up on us from behind, above, or below, but if that thing finds us, corners us in here, we'll be trapped. I sit in front of the entrance. Whatever's down here will have to go through me first.

"Why?" Maria asks, fighting back tears. "Darryl was kind . . . he never hurt anyone. He was a gentle giant . . . you know that."

"I do," Shy says as she cradles Maria against her.

"All he wanted to do was graduate. Serve his country. Get married. Have kids. The white picket fence."

I try to keep the image out of my head, but I can picture it, clear as day. It hurts to think of everything Darryl lost. What the world lost without him in it.

"And this is how it ends? Cold and wet and dark, with his head bashed in?" Maria shivers at the memory. "I'm all alone now."

"You're not alone," Shy says. "We have each other."

"For how much longer? Whatever that thing is . . . it's picking us off, one by one."

"We don't know that."

"You saw what it did to Darryl. It just picked him up off the ground, smashed him against the rock, and threw him back down again . . . like it was nothing. Could a man even do that?" She lets out a shuddering breath. "What if Darryl's right? What if it's some kind of animal . . . or something *else*?"

"Shh . . ." Shy says as she strokes her hair.

"It reminds me of that special we watched in Earth Science last year. Remember? The one on the orca whales? I always thought they were so cute, but then I saw them tossing those seals around, back and forth. They were playing with their food before they ate it. They were having fun. What if something's down here . . . playing with *us*?"

"You need sleep," Shy says as she gets Maria to lie down in her lap. "When we're done with this place, we're going to figure everything out. You can cry and wail and fall apart, but right now, we have one job."

"Survive," I say.

Maria looks over at me, her eyes full of pain and blame and regret. I can't stand to have her look at me that way.

"I feel like I'm going crazy," she whispers. "Do you think maybe we're all going crazy?"

As soon as she closes her eyes, I finally feel like I can breathe again. I can't imagine what that would be like, watching the person you love die.

"Is Maria going to be okay?" I ask.

"She's been through a lot." Shy leans her head back against the rock wall. "Her older brother died when she was eight . . . right in her arms."

"Was he sick?"

"Drive-by."

"Oh." I glance at Maria. "Was he into drugs?"

"Is that how you think of us?" she snaps.

"No," I say, recoiling from her words a bit. "I'm sorry if that came out wrong. I just . . . I don't know . . . I don't know anything anymore."

She takes a deep breath and her face softens. "That wasn't fair. Sometimes I forget that I don't have to fight so hard all the time. They're just poor. Wrong neighborhood. Wrong time. Took the ambulance an hour to show up. That's when she got into the EMT thing. She wanted to help people. Give back to the community."

"I can see that." I clench my jaw.

"What? What is it?"

"I was just thinking about my friends. The people I grew up with. Sure, they'll donate to get their name on some plaque, buy a wristband to support whatever cause of the day, but I've never heard a single one of them talk passionately about how they want to help people—and then actually do something about it. Except my sister, Mare. She doesn't talk about helping people. She just does it."

"Your sister sounds nice," she says with a weary smile. "Maybe you can do the same. It's not too late for you, you know."

I want to tell Shy how I feel, how I can't stop thinking

about her. Even down here, with death and madness all around us, all I want to do is be close to her, but I can feel my cheeks getting red just thinking about it.

"What about your family?" I ask, pretending to reorganize the supplies.

There's a hesitation, and I think she's going to blow me off, but she starts talking.

"I live with my grandma."

"Ruth, right? The harpist?"

"You remembered."

"Of course," I reply, trying not to sound too eager. "What happened to your parents?"

"My dad's down at Red Onion. Never getting out. My mom got into crack."

"I'm sorry. Did she pass?"

"No." She wraps her arms around herself. "But sometimes it's easier to think of her that way. She lives in Richmond. I see her now and then. She used to come around. She'd sit on the couch and cry, braid my hair. I couldn't understand it at the time. If she wanted me so much, if I meant that much to her, why couldn't she take me with her? I made up every excuse you can possibly imagine when she didn't show. I was always defending her to everyone. But there were times when she'd show up looking for money. She didn't want to braid my hair. She didn't even want to look at me. I used to tell myself she had a twin sister—an evil twin—but I knew the truth."

She stares past me, into the dark. "I felt bad about it, the lowest you can feel, but my grandma taught me right."

She sits up a little straighter. "Got me involved in sports, church. Made sure I was where I was supposed to be at all times. It was annoying, especially in middle school, her telling me who I could and couldn't be friends with, but she was right."

She pulls her ponytail over her shoulder. "She tolerated Kit hanging around, because he was harmless, he made her laugh, and she knew he didn't have anybody. But when other boys started coming around . . . forget it. She even chased one of them off our steps with a rake. Can you imagine?" She smiles, but it quickly fades.

"Now, she's in and out." She swallows hard. "Alzheimer's. Some days she remembers me, sometimes she thinks I'm my mom. Some days she thinks I've broken in and I'm trying to rob the place. But on the good days," she says as she leans forward, "it doesn't get any better than that. Like going to the tree-lighting ceremony. She's always trying to show me a better life. I remember looking at you, your sister, your parents, thinking how perfect your life must be. You had on this dark-blue wool coat with six buttons. You were all matching. Like dolls at the store. It was like someone just pulled you out of a package and set you on stage."

"I guess you didn't see the big zit right in the middle of my forehead then? My mom had her makeup artist working on that thing for at least an hour."

"Well . . . you couldn't tell."

"You'll have to tell her it was a big success. She works really hard to project that image."

She gets quiet, and I know she's thinking about what's going to happen when we get out of here.

"My mom's going to love you. She's strong, like you."

"That's a crazy thought." She sinks into the rock a little deeper. "Me, sitting down with your mom. Having tea."

"Why not?" I look around our cramped quarters. "Stranger things have happened."

"Sometimes I wonder how we got here," she says, her brow furrowing up. "I made good grades, stayed out of trouble, worked hard, and then something like this happens and you think . . . what's it all for? I believe in God. I do. I believe everything happens for a reason. But, for the life of me, I can't figure this one out. What good could possibly come from all this? Kit's dead. Darryl's dead. Us being trapped down here with some kind of killer . . . some kind of *monster*," she says with a shivering breath.

"I'm going to get you out of here. We're going to make it. We have to."

I don't know if it's lack of sleep, lack of food, the cold, or the dark, but I feel myself slipping. I don't want to fall asleep, but I'm so tired.

Shy reaches out to touch my face. Her hands feel like cool marble gliding across my feverish skin, her soft brown eyes piercing right through me. I've never met anyone like her. She's struggled her whole life, but look at her . . . she's amazing. She held me together down here. All of us. And as I stare into her eyes, I decide right then and there that if we get out of here, I'm going to follow her to the ends of the earth. And if she won't have me,

I'm going to do everything in my power to make her life easier . . . to show her the kindness she showed me, that she showed every single one of us down here. She's tough, but I can see right through her, too, and she's breathtaking.

"Sleep," she whispers.

23

WHEN I open my eyes, I'm alone.

It's so dark I'm not even sure if I'm a person anymore or a spirit floating through the ether. I wonder if this is how it starts . . . how the rapture sets in.

But then I remember Shy and Maria.

I reach for my headlamp. It's gone.

In a panic, I call out their names.

A flashlight turns on and they sit up, groggily rubbing their eyes.

"Hey." I let out a heavy sigh. It's so cold you can see my breath. "They were just lying down, that's all," I say to myself.

"Are you okay?" Shy asks.

"Yeah. I don't know. I think it was just a nightmare."

"Here, you need to drink." Shy lifts the water bottle to my cracked lips. It's hard to swallow at first, like my throat forgot how, but after a few sips, it feels a little more natural. I don't even taste the dirt anymore.

"And you need to eat. You still have some ice cream left."

"I'm okay. Really."

"If you pass out . . . if you die . . . we're never getting out of here. You need to be strong for Maria, and Kit, and Darryl. Be strong for me."

"Okay." I take the last freeze-dried bite, letting it melt in my mouth, down my throat, but it only seems to anger my hollow stomach.

As we pack up and trudge deeper into the tunnel, every drip, every scattering stone, has us completely on edge.

I'm thinking anything would be better than this. Being lost at sea. Stranded in the woods. It's the unknown that scares me the most—the darkness right beyond the reach of our light, where anything could be waiting for us.

"Did you remember more?" Shy asks, her voice startling me. "Is that what the nightmares are about?"

I clear my throat. "From the incident?"

"The incident?"

"Yeah, sorry, that's what everyone calls it. They whisper it like it's a dirty word."

"Like *Voldemort,*" she says with a smile. When I don't

smile back, she says, "It was an accident, Grant. People make mistakes."

"Not like this." I swallow hard. "I try not to go there, but sometimes I think, what if I just walked in on Lewis and Catherine and gave them my blessing. Or if I just turned a blind eye, and let those guys break into his parents' wine cellar. Or if I didn't have that second shot. Or if I didn't go to the party at all—"

"We all play *what ifs,*" Shy says. "But it won't change anything. Yeah, you shouldn't have been driving, and maybe you were a jerk before, but I don't know that person. The Grant I know is kind . . . and damaged. But not broken. You can fix this. You can do the right thing. Until you accept what happened, face it, you'll never be able to live. But I believe in you."

Her words seem to cut right through me, to the heart of the matter.

Because if someone like Shy can believe in someone like me, I can't be that bad.

When we come around the bend in the rock we see that the tunnel is completely submerged in a dark, murky pool of water. My heart sinks.

"Darryl was right." Maria tears up as she stares at the glassy surface. "We're all going to die down here."

"No we're not," Shy says. "There has to be a way. Right, Grant?"

I take a deep breath, trying not to freak out, when I get a whiff. *Guano.* Grabbing the flashlight, I search the cavern for the bats. I'm starting to think I might be hal-lucinating the smell, until I spot a long, narrow slit in the stone above the submerged tunnel. It's not big enough for us to squeeze through, but it's big enough for the bats.

I start taking off my clothes.

"What are you doing?" Shy lets out a nervous laugh.

"I'm going in." I can't look up at her or I might lose my nerve. "And if I get my clothes wet, I'm as good as dead down here." When I open the emergency kit to take out the dry pouch, I see a glow stick. I'm so happy to see it that I give it a kiss.

"If I can find a way through—"

"Wait." Shy steps in front of me. "You can't just dive in there and leave us here . . . not without a plan."

"I'm just going to see how far it goes. It could be a quick duck to the other side."

"You're not thinking straight. We have to be smart. How long can you hold your breath?"

"Probably forty-five seconds."

"So that means at twenty seconds you have to turn back," she says as she grabs a rope out my bag. "And I'm tying this around your waist in case you forget how to count."

When I step into the freezing water, I have to clench my jaw so I don't cry out. If there's someone down here hunting us, the last thing I want to do is draw attention to our location. I look down into the stagnant pool, try-ing to get my footing. I don't even want to think about what else is living in here. Darryl told me about some microbe in a submerged cave in Belize that goes into every orifice, looking for a host. That would be just my luck. Survive a cave collapse, and a monstrous killer, only to die three days later from a rare brain-eating microbe. But I can't think about Darryl right now. I can't think about dying. Maria and Shy are counting on me.

I crack the light stick, which emits only a soft glow, but it's better than nothing.

Diving into murky water practically naked with only a light stick is crazy, but if I don't do this—if I don't find a way out—we'll die, either from starvation or at the hands of whatever it is that's hunting us down here. And after everything that's happened, I refuse to go down like that.

I take one last look at them, huddling on the muddy bank, dirt and grime covering their faces, and I get the saddest feeling. Even if we make it out of here, they'll never be the same. Kit's gone. Darryl's gone. But beneath the filth, beneath the horror, we still have fight in us. We're still here.

I take three deep breaths and then duck under the surface. The shock to my system feels almost paralyzing, but then I think about what's at stake and push forward. The salinity in the water won't let me sink, and without weights or flippers, I have very little control. Even with the light stick, I can only see a few inches in front of my face. My eyes burn with the strain of keeping them open. I kick as hard as I can, but the dark water feels thick, like I'm swimming through gelatin. For all I know, this sump could go on for a mile. Even a foot beyond my lung capacity will be too far.

I don't know if it's the grim thoughts, the muscle fatigue, or the cold, but it's slowing me down. I can't even feel my limbs anymore.

Bashing into a rock, I drop the light stick. I reach out to reclaim it, but it seems to drift right through my fingers. Or maybe my hands aren't working anymore. I try to go after it, but as the glow disappears, I quickly become disoriented, forgetting which way is up and which way is down.

Panicking, I reach out for anything I can grab hold of. When my knuckles bash into jagged rock, I grasp onto it with hungry fingers, pulling myself along, like something straight out of a horror movie, until my lips find a pocket of air. I take every last bit into my lungs, hoping it's not just an air bell with pure carbon dioxide poisoning my body, but as I pull myself farther, I realize it's not just an air bell but a way out. I've reached the other side.

I have zero visibility, no way of knowing what this space is like, but it feels vast.

"Hello," I whisper, and the cave whispers back. But it's more than that. There's a faint squeaking, along with what sounds like the occasional thrum of beating wings. The bats. They must be close.

I feel a breeze brush against my freezing skin and I know there's air moving through here. Either that, or the killer is standing right beside me, breathing on me.

Just as I work up the nerve to swipe the air in front of

me, I'm jerked back under water. I try to hang on to the rocks, but Shy's too strong. The best thing I can do at this point is let go.

I try to protect myself, but I'm dragged against the rock ceiling the entire way back.

As I break through the surface, Shy's yelling, "What happened? I told you to swim back after twenty seconds. Wait," she says as she shines the light on my face. "You're bleeding."

I feel my head. There's blood, but I think it's just a scrape from when she pulled me back. "It's nothing. Listen . . . I lost the glow stick, but there's a cavern."

"Did you see light?" she asks, the mere thought making her short of breath.

"No. But I think I heard the bats. The surface can't be far."

"Did you hear that, Maria?"

We turn to find Maria rocking on the ground, staring at the water with a haunted look on her face.

"I can't go," she whispers.

"Why would you say that?" Shy steps toward her. "If this is about Darryl–"

"No, Darryl would want me to survive." She looks up at Shy, her eyes full of tears. "But . . . I . . . I can't swim."

"It's okay," I tell her. "You don't have to swim. I'm going to set up a rope and all you have to do is hold your breath and pull yourself along."

Shy kneels down, putting her arm around Maria, talking to her quietly as I drill an anchor into the rock wall and tie off the rope. I'm shaking so hard from the cold that I can hardly find a grip.

"I'll have to go over first with the supplies," I explain. "It will take me a few minutes to light the candle, set up the anchor, but when I pull on the rope three times, that's your signal. The sump will only take about thirty seconds to get through—probably less with the guide rope."

"Grant, I just—"

"It's going to be okay. We can do this."

"No." She looks up at me, her eyes shining in the dull light. "I just wanted to thank you for doing all this. For trying to save us." The warmth in her voice nearly brings me to my knees.

"I'm the one who should be thanking you. Finding me, the way you did," I say as I take her hands in mine. "It might be the luckiest thing that's ever happened to me."

For a second I think maybe she's going to kiss me, like Leia kissed Luke on the Death Star, right before they swung across that bridge, but then I remember that they were brother and sister, and I don't want Shy to kiss me that way. I want her to kiss me like Leia kissed Han right before he's frozen in carbonite. And I can't even believe this is what I'm thinking about right now. My fever must be coming back with a vengeance.

Maria starts coughing, and Shy lets go of my hands.

Busying myself with the pack, I make sure the supplies I need are easy to find. "I'm leaving you in charge of the flashlight," I say as I seal it in a Ziploc and hand it to her.

"But I'm going to need your clothes. I know it's freezing, but it's vital that we have—"

Without the slightest hesitation, Shy starts peeling off her sweatshirt, and I quickly turn away.

As they hand me their clothes over my shoulder, Shy says, "You don't have to be such a gentleman all the time. I think we're beyond that now."

"I don't know if I'll ever be beyond that with you," I say as I seal everything up.

Getting in the pool of water, I'm surprised that it feels warm to me now. That's not a good sign. I submerge the bag and glance up at her one last time.

She's standing there in her underwear; her long legs seem to go on forever.

Feeling the heat rush to my cheeks, I duck under the water.

For once, I'm glad for the dark.

It's harder getting across with the rope and bag in tow, but I know what to expect now. Unspooling the rope as I go, I inch forward into pure darkness. It's so disorienting, there are moments when I forget what I'm doing, why I'm even down here, but then I think of Shy and Maria back there, shivering on the water's edge, and that's enough to keep me going . . . to keep me striving for air.

As soon as I resurface, I crawl my way onto the bank. Setting down the pack, I pull out the candle and the box of matches. I'm shaking so hard I can barely manage to grab hold of one.

But as I sit there, poised to strike, a wave of fear comes over me.

Maybe I don't want to see what this place really is. The foul odor, the strange sounds . . . what if it's not the bats but the monster's lair? A cavern full of skinned snakes, severed bat wings, and rib cages dangling like chandeliers, from all his victims?

And as soon as the thought creeps into my consciousness, it's all I can think about.

I squint into the dark, and I swear I can see someone in my peripheral—a white, shadowy figure, faceless, without form, darting around the vast space. My heart's pounding. A deep thick thrum pulsing in my ears.

I force myself to close my eyes, quiet my thoughts, and when I open them again there's nothing but darkness, water, and cold.

Whatever's happening down here, I can't give in to the fear. Not now. Not when we're this close.

I strike a flame, quickly lighting the wick.

In the dim light, I see a giant slab of limestone precariously balanced over the sump. Highly unstable. This whole thing could come down at any moment. But above it all, I see the most beautiful sight in the world.

Bats. Hundreds of them, hanging upside down from the ceiling. It must be daytime. What day, I have no idea, but all we have to do is wait until it's feeding time and follow them out.

"*Out,*" I whisper, my eyes welling up with tears.

Hurrying to the side of the submerged tunnel, I carefully set up the anchor and pull on the rope three times to let them know I'm ready.

As I crouch in front of the water, I count . . . and wait.

Thirty seconds go by and I'm starting to get nervous. I hop back in the water, but I'm so cold I don't even feel it anymore. Another ten seconds pass, and I'm about to go in after them, when Shy breaks through the surface, gasping for air.

"Shh," I whisper as I point to the ceiling.

"Whoa," she says, panning the flashlight over the scene. "Wait. Where's Maria? She went first."

We turn our lights on the water. As soon as I see Maria surface, I blow out the candle and start getting everything ready to go, but something's not right. Maria's splashing around, grasping at Shy. She's trying to say something, but she can't find the air.

"You have to calm her down," I say, keeping an eye on the bats as they're becoming increasingly more agitated.

"Please, Maria, breathe. Slow down. I'm here. What is it?"

"I . . . I felt something down there. I felt something pull my hair," she says as she grabs onto Shy, holding her tight.

"It probably just got snagged on the rocks. That's all. We're safe now, and look . . ." She points to the ceiling. "We found the bats. They're going to lead us out of here."

Maria looks up, a weary smile easing over her blue lips. "Thank God," she whispers. Clasping her hands under her chin, she starts to climb out of the pool—when she disappears under the water with a violent splash.

Shy and I look at each other, confusion quickly turning to panic.

I jump back in. Shy and I are frantically searching the water for any sign of her when Maria's head pops back up.

"Jesus, Maria." Shy puts her hand to her chest. "What did you do, trip? You scared me."

But when Shy tries to help her up, there's nothing but water where her body should be.

With a shaky hand, Shy reaches out to touch a strand of Maria's hair.

Her head rolls toward us—completely severed—eyes wide open as if she'd just seen a monster.

"Not again," I say, the horror of what I'm seeing slowly spreads through my body, making my joints lock up.

Shy staggers out of the water, her hands held up in front of her as if they're covered in blood. "We have to go," she murmurs. "We can't stay here."

A splashing sound, coming from the left, seems to suck all the air from my lungs. "Who's there?" I whisper.

It whispers back. I can't make out the words, but I can feel it coming toward me. Seeking me out.

"Grant, please," Shy says, tugging on my arm.

I pull away, raising the flashlight. There's a long, sinewy shadow lurking at the water's edge, but I can't figure out where it's coming from.

"We have to go," she says, pulling harder.

I'm leaning forward, desperate to see what it is, what kind of monster could've done this, when Shy yanks me out of the water. "If we stay here, we'll die!"

The shrill echo triggers the bats.

As they take off en masse, the cacophony of screeches and beating wings swells to a feverish pitch.

Grabbing the bag, we chase after them. The entire cavern trembles beneath our feet. I know it's just the limestone collapsing in our wake, but it feels like the killer is breathing right down our necks.

Playing with us.

24

WE follow the bats as long as we can, but they're too fast.

Or we're too slow.

I don't know if it's the shock or the cold, but it feels like we're still moving under icy water.

"Light," Shy says, pulling me into a narrow crevice. "Do you see it?"

At first I think it's just our senses playing tricks on us, but as we get closer it's undeniable . . . there's something glowing up ahead.

We pick up our pace. My heart's beating so hard I'm afraid it might burst through my chest, but when I place my hand over it I can barely feel it pumping.

"I think it might be moonlight," she pants. "This is it. We're going to make it."

As soon as we reach the cavern, I realize this is something else entirely.

"I don't understand," Shy says, shining the flashlight over the long strands of strange blue lights dangling from the ceiling.

I sink to the ground, staring up into the abyss, a sense of awe washing over me.

> *"Venus lies star-struck in her wound*
> *And the sensual ruins make*
> *Seasons over the liquid world,*
> *White springs in the dark,"* I murmur.

"Grant, look at me." Shy's shaking my shoulders.

"Dylan Thomas."

"Stop it. You're scaring me," she says, slapping me repeatedly on the cheek, but I hardly feel it. "You can't give up."

I blink hard, the world slowly coming back into focus, the slight sting returning to my cheek. "They're glow-worms," I whisper. "I've never seen one in real life, but I heard about a cave in Alabama that has a cavern like this. Definitely not in the Crystal Falls guidebook."

"So we have to keep going," she says as she tries to pull me back up, but my legs won't work anymore.

"I don't know if it's real," I say, taking in a slow, deep

breath, "but I swear I can smell soil and clay. Damp leaves . . . and sunshine. If I close my eyes, it's almost like I can feel it warming my skin."

"You're not cold?" Shy asks.

I think about it for a long time. Too long. "No." I manage to shrug. "Are you?"

"No."

"Maybe we've just gotten used to it down here," I say, my eyelids getting heavy.

"Or maybe we're freezing to death," she says as she digs through the pack. "Maria said that was the second phase of hypothermia."

"We should put on our clothes . . ."

"It's too late for that now." Shy pulls out the heat bag. "Skin on skin. You said that was the quickest way."

"I was kind of kidding. We don't have to do that. We can take turns."

"Don't make me beg you to cuddle," she says.

I crack a weak smile.

"Here, let's get you in first," she says as she puts my legs in the bag. "If I sit on your lap, facing you, we'll both be able to keep a lookout."

As she settles on my lap, wrapping her legs around me, I'm thinking maybe this isn't the worst way to go. They'll find us someday, in one last final embrace. Write poems about us.

"Is this okay?" she asks.

"Normally, this would be the most exciting thing in the

world." I smile into her collarbone. "But unfortunately, I can't feel anything."

Shy pulls the bag up around our shoulders and wraps her arms around me.

We breathe into the bag, trapping the warm air inside. It takes awhile, but as soon as the shivering sets back in, so do the feelings.

"Maria," Shy whispers. I feel her scalding tears against my back.

"I'm so sorry." I hold her tighter. "I'm sorry this happened to you. To any of you. You don't deserve this."

"But you think you do?" she asks softly.

I let out a shuddering breath. "You wouldn't even be down here if it wasn't for me. I'm the one who caused all this. Do you ever think that maybe all of this was meant for me? That you just wandered into my bad karma? Wrong place. Wrong time. It's all so unfair."

"Nothing's fair. Take a look at your hand," she says as she pulls mine forward. "Your fingers. They're all different sizes. Some are crooked, some are straight. Nothing's equal in this world."

I close my hand around hers and breathe into it. She still feels so cold.

"They almost look like shooting stars," she says as she looks up at the ceiling. "Maybe we should make a wish."

I try to look up, play along, but I can't seem to take my eyes off Shy. "I wish we'd met sooner," I say. "I wish when you were at that tree-lighting ceremony you would've come up to me and shook me and said, 'Wake up, V.'"

"Would you have heard me?" she says softly. "Would you have even seen me?"

I brush a stray curl away from her neck. "How could I not see you?"

"If we get out of here—"

"*When* we get out of here," I correct her.

"I want you to promise me something."

"Anything."

She leans back so she can look me straight in the eyes, the soft blue light creating this ethereal glow around her. "Don't let their deaths be for nothing. Instead of turning all that guilt inward, let it out for the world to see. You owe that to Kit, Darryl, and Maria. You owe it to me." She laces her fingers through mine, and I get goose bumps, but not because I'm cold. "I know why this happened now," she says, resting her forehead against mine. "It's because you and I were meant to meet, in one way or another. I believe everything happens for a reason, don't you?"

"I do now."

As I lean in to kiss her, I've never been so sure about something and so scared at the same time.

The touch of her lips.

The feel of her skin.

There's no nervous fumbling or awkward angles. It's all soft and warm and deep. She presses even closer, and I feel like I might disappear into her. I've never felt so connected to anyone in my entire life. It doesn't feel like a first kiss.

Somehow, it feels like the last.

And if we don't find a way out of here soon, it very well could be.

As she pulls away, I know exactly what she's going to say. "It's time," she whispers.

The last thing I want to do is separate from her, but I know she's right. And I'd trade a million dark, dreamy kisses for one kiss under the sun, out in the open.

25

HAND in hand, we descend deeper into the cave. There are occasional faint squeaking noises, fluttering wings, but it's impossible to tell how close they are. It could be twenty feet or a mile away, but all we have to do at this point is stay alive long enough to find them again.

"So tell me," Shy says. "What is it about poetry that you like so much?"

It takes me aback. I don't think anyone's ever asked me that before. "Look, I'm sorry if I freaked you out. It's just a thing I do when—"

"No. It's not that." She squeezes my hand. "I'm just curious."

I take in a deep breath. "It's hard to explain. I mean,

they're just words, right? Everyday words that we take for granted, but when you put them together with care and purpose, they can be transformed into something magical."

"I get that," Shy says as she bites down gently on her bottom lip. "I guess that's kind of how I feel about the truth." She glances up at me. "The truth shall set you free, right?"

I stare ahead at the darkness before us. "I haven't felt free in a long time," I say. "Maybe ever."

"You can change that," she says as she pulls me to a stop.

"I hope so. I hope I get that chance." I meet her eyes, wishing she would kiss me again.

"On a completely different subject," she says with a sheepish smile, "I have to . . . you know."

"Now?" I ask. "But I think we're getting really close."

"It's all this dripping." She laughs as she looks around for a private spot.

"Seriously." I let out a long sigh. "It's funny how I thought it was soothing when I first got down here, but now it's like Chinese water torture."

"This will work," she says, pointing to a huge flowstone formation.

She tries to let go of my hand, but I hang on. "You're crazy if you think I'm leaving you alone, even for a second."

"I can't pee in front of you."

"Amateur," I tease. "I can stand on the other side of this rock, but you have to hold my hand the entire time."

"This is so weird," she says as she steps behind the stone and starts bouncing around, messing with her track pants.

"Oh, I think we're beyond weird at this point."

"Just keep talking," she says. I can tell she's uncomfortable by the way she's breathing.

"I got used to peeing in front of people," I explain. "I had to do drug testing for three months, once a week. Mostly it was the same nurse. This guy, Benny. He had this tattoo on his wrist that—"

There's a weird ripping sound, followed by a gush of liquid.

It makes me wince, but I try to make her feel better. "Please don't be embarrassed. The water we've been drinking, it probably has a ton of microbes in it. That can really mess with your stomach. Not to mention all we've had to eat is little bits of astronaut food. That's bound to turn anyone's stomach sour."

But all I hear is dripping. It's thundering in my ears.

"Shy?"

When she doesn't reply, I look down at our hands. They're still entwined, but there's a trail of blood seeping down her arm, into the palm of my hand.

I blink hard, hoping it's just an illusion. The dark playing tricks on me again.

But when I look around the corner I see that I'm holding her severed arm.

"Shy?" I scream, swinging the flashlight around the cavern wildly.

I catch a trail of blood glistening in the dark. It leads me deeper into the tunnel.

"Please let this be a hallucination . . . Not her. Please, not her," I say.

When I stumble upon the rest of her body, I know it's real.

She's curled up on the ground in the strangest position. Her eyes are wide and clear. It's that same hollow look she always gets . . . that same expression I can never decipher.

"Shy." I lie down next to her and kiss her forehead, the one place that doesn't look like it hurts. "Was it the monster?"

She blinks, and I know she's telling me yes.

"Is he here now?"

She blinks again.

"I know I said I'd never hurt anyone again," I say through trembling lips, "but I'm going to kill that thing."

She blinks again.

"But first, I have to get you out of here."

She doesn't blink this time.

As I reach in to try and scoop her up, she grips onto me. Her lips are moving, but I don't hear a sound. Leaning in close, I'm desperate to hear her voice, desperate to hear what she has to say.

I press my ear to her lips, and the flashlight flickers once.

Twice.

A third time.

Until it's finally extinguished.

"No." I shake them both, as if I can bring them back to life. Tears are streaming down my face as I hug her to my chest, rocking back and forth, humming that Mozart melody, but I know she's gone.

I don't know how long I stay frozen like this. Minutes. Hours. Days. I've lost sense of everything around me . . . who I am.

It's pitch black—so dark that I'm not even sure if I'm holding her anymore. I'm not even sure if I have arms anymore. I can hear my breath . . . hear the incessant dripping that's become my constant companion . . . But there's something else, a presence all around me, taunting me, as if it's daring me to get up and face it.

I have a choice. I can either cower in the dark, wait for it to take me, or I can stand up and kill it—or die trying. My father said this trip would make a man out of me.

And he was right.

"I know why you saved me for last," I say as I grab the candle and matches from my bag. "You wanted me to suffer as much as humanly possible." I rattle around the box of matches to find there's only one left.

I have to make this count.

"So here I am," I say as I strike the match.

Phosphorous and charcoal flares in my nostrils.

My hands are shaking, but I manage to light the wick.

"I'm all alone now. Come and get me," I whisper.

As I stand and walk into the darkness, I weep not for myself but for the people I killed in that accident, for my family and friends that I left behind, for Kit, Darryl, Maria, and Shy.

Just thinking about how they died, like they were nothing, makes me so enraged I feel like I could tear down the entire cave with my bare hands.

"What are you waiting for," I call out. "I'm right here." I take another step and I hear something. The whisper swirling all around me, like a serpent waiting to strike.

"Come and face me like a man," I scream into the tunnel.

The tunnel screams back.

I rock back on my heels, trembling with fear. I'm not sure if it's the monster or my own voice echoing back, but it registers in every molecule of my body. I've heard that sound before.

Tires screeching across pavement. Metal, glass, asphalt colliding.

And it's coming right toward me.

I brace myself for impact, facing it head-on.

The whoosh of the incoming horror blows out the flame, and I know this is it. The moment of reckoning.

The moment of truth.

Exactly what I deserve.

But it's only the bats, barreling through the cavern, shooting over me, straight up into the heavens above.

Staggering after them, I stare up to see a narrow chute, hazy shafts of light filtering through a thick veil of moss.

I take in a gasping breath of air. It feels like a miracle, like this was their souls breaking free, showing me the way.

Crawling after it, I claw my way toward the light. Every inch gained, I think of Shy and Maria, Darryl and Kit. They lost their lives on this journey, but I can still make things right.

I lose my footing and skid down a few inches, but I manage to hang on. As much as my muscles are screaming at me to let go, I push past the fatigue, the cold, the numbness in my legs, and will my body to move. Grabbing onto roots and vines, I dig in my heels. Each step is harder than the last. My muscles are burning, my hands are blistering under the strain, but I keep going. I hear the monster behind me, right on my heels, breathing down my neck, but I don't look back. I keep digging . . . reaching for higher ground . . . for everything they wanted their lives to be.

And when my hand breaks through the surface and the light comes spilling in, I have to clench my eyes shut, because it hurts so much.

"Over here!" someone hollers.

As hands clasp onto me, pulling me from the bowels of the earth, I'm waiting for the monster to grab my ankle, to drag me back into the depths of hell. But all I feel is fresh air . . . sunlight on my skin. As grateful as I am, I wish Shy could feel this. I wish they were all with me now.

"Grant Tavish . . . is that you?"

"Yes," I manage to reply through cracked lips, but it feels like I haven't used my vocal cords in days. "The bats led me out."

They give me a strange look before waving around a flag.

People are running toward me from all directions—police, rescue workers. There are tents set up all over the place, a sea of news cameras behind a barricade, helicopters whirring overhead.

As soon as my eyes fully adjust, I look back at the narrow fissure in the rock from where I escaped, and it seems impossible.

For a minute, I wonder if this is even real. What if I'm still stuck down there, alone, starving in the dark, freezing to death, and all of this is just some elaborate hallucination to help ease me into death?

But when I see my mom, dad, and sister running up the hill, the anguished looks on their faces, I know this is real.

And that, somehow, I'm alive.

26

"WE'RE here, son," my father says, trying to hide the tears in his eyes.

My mother hugs me, really hugs me. "Thank God you're okay," she whispers in my ear.

My sister just stands there crying, like it hurts to even look at me.

"I'm so sorry," I manage to get out, before completely breaking down.

We all hug at the same time, something we've never done before, and as much as I want to bask in this moment, I can't stop thinking about Kit, Darryl, Maria, and Shy. Where's their welcome party? Where's their family reunion?

"We've got him," one of the officers says into his radio, unable to contain his excitement. "He's alive. You can call off the search."

I hear cheering from the bottom of the hill, where the barricade is set up.

"Wait," I blurt. "You can't call it off. They're still down there."

"Who's still down there?" the officer asks.

"Kit, Maria, Darryl, and Shy," I answer, my chin quivering. "I tried to save them. I tried to get them out, but there's something down there. Something evil. The things he did to them . . . the way they died . . . it was a massacre."

"He must be delirious," my mother says.

"Can we get medical up here?" my dad calls out.

The paramedics race up the hill with a stretcher and immediately start checking my body for any signs of injury, my vitals, reflexes.

"Are you listening to me?" I say. "The rescue team has to know what they're dealing with before they go dow—"

"Mostly surface wounds, trauma to the left shoulder," the paramedic talks over me. "But he's definitely dehydrated and there's signs of hypothermia," he says as he drapes a blanket around me.

"There's nothing wrong with me." I stand up.

They start to pull me back down, but my father signals them to stay back. "Grant, talk to me. Are you saying there were other people down there with you?"

"Yes, there were five of us. They were part of the school

group. They were in the drop when the collapse happened. It's my fault they got stuck down there in the first place."

"Has anyone else been reported missing?" my father asks the officer.

"No." He checks his notebook. "Not a soul."

"No one from the school group?" my father asks. "Are you sure?"

"One hundred percent," the officer replies. "Everyone's accounted for."

"They must've made a mistake," I say. "It was chaotic. There were kids running all over the place. They go to Richmond Central. Maybe they weren't on the official list, but I know who I was down there with. Wait . . . I remember they drove. Shy borrowed her grandma's car and—"

"We might want to get him to the hospital," the officer says sympathetically. "He could be in shock, or have a head injury."

"Dad, please . . ."

He looks me in the eyes and gives a slight nod. "If my son says there are people down there, you need to take this seriously."

"Of course, Senator Tavish," he says, immediately backing down.

I almost feel sorry for the cop, but this is too important.

He gets on his radio. "We've got a possible recovery situation. Four bodies. Can you send up the NCRC team?"

As three rugged-looking guys come up the hill, decked out in full gear, I know they're the real deal.

The officer goes to speak with them before bringing them over, but I can tell these guys are aching for a reason to go down there. They'll hear me out.

"Can you give us names? Descriptions?" the officer asks as he pulls out his pen.

"Yeah . . . yeah, of course I can." I gather the wool blanket tighter around my neck. "Kit Jackson, but his real name is Jeremiah George Jackson. He's thin, smart. He's in foster care . . . he stays with a woman named June. There's Darryl James Arnold, about six two, buzz cut. He lives in the trailer park off Meadow Lane. Maria Priscilla Perez, long, straight hair, bangs, around five foot four— she's in EMT training. And then there's Shy. Shyanne Rose Taylor." Even saying her name out loud hurts. "Dark curly hair, tall. She's an athlete. Discus. All-state. She lives with her grandma Ruth. She has Olympic trials on Monday." I swallow hard. "She *had* Olympic trials on Monday."

I look up and the officer's not even writing this down anymore. They're all just standing there, a sea of confusion on their faces. I look to my family for support, but they're huddled together. They can't even look me in the eyes.

"Why aren't you writing this down? Why aren't you doing anything? You need to send a team down there to get their bodies. They deserve a funeral. But I'm telling you, the rescue team needs protection, backup, because whatever's down there . . . it's not human. Not anymore."

"The rapture," one of the rescuers whispers.

"The what?" the cop asks.

"It's a caving term. It can happen in extreme conditions. It's when you hallucinate from sensory deprivation."

"You don't have to whisper. I can hear you," I say. "I know all about that. And that's not what's going on here. They found me, they rescued me. We had to pass through a chamber full of guano and cockroaches, a squeeze so tight they had to dislocate my shoulder to get me through. I couldn't have done all that by myself."

A deputy hands a newspaper to my dad; he looks at it and nods.

"What?" I ask. "What is it?"

As my dad places the paper in my hands, he puts his arm around me. I'm not sure if he's trying to steady me or himself. "Are these the kids you're talking about?"

I look at the paper, and there they are, on the front page, all lined up. It's their school photos. And next to it there's a big photo of me, pre-incident, looking like I don't have a care in the world.

"Yes." I run my finger over Shy's face. "So you know about them?"

"Read the headline," my father says gently.

"Senator's son, Grant Tavish V, still missing.

"You may remember him from the gruesome accident that killed four Richmond Central High School teens this past December."

It starts in my fingers, a chill so deep it travels through my entire body, turning my bones to brittle ice.

I step away from the crowd, staring into the narrow crack in the limestone, and suddenly I'm back to that night, staring down at the gash in the pavement. As I walk toward the wreckage, all I want to do is close my eyes, but I force myself to look . . . to face the truth of what I've done.

I see Kit, clutching his red flashlight, the DEER CROSS-ING sign impaled through his chest.

I see Darryl, his skull crushed against the pavement, his fingertips flickering.

I see Maria, decapitated on the side of the road, the snow melting around her.

And then I see Shy, hanging halfway through the windshield, her arm resting at my feet. She's staring right at me. Her mouth is moving, but I can't hear what she's saying.

I step closer.

There's glass crunching beneath the soles of my shoes.

Closer.

I crouch next to her, pressing my ear against her lips.

"You're the monster," she whispers.

I stagger back, reality crashing back down on me like a giant boulder.

Falling to my knees, I press my palms against the hard, unforgiving earth.

That's why all of our watches stopped at 11:57. The time of the accident. That's why they were always colder than me, but they never needed to warm up. That's why we were able to pass the food around so many times, because I was the only one eating it. That's why Darryl was able to get through that squeeze so easily and I wasn't. And that look Shy always had, that sad, hollow look like she knew how this was all going to end—that's the same look she gave me from behind the steering wheel, when I crashed into her grandma's car that night.

They were the best friends I ever had, and I killed them.

"Let's get you home," my father says as he steps behind me, placing his hands on my shoulders. "You've been through a terrible ordeal. You just need time. Rest. But soon this will be nothing but a faint memory."

A glimmer of light hits my face, an errant ray of sunshine, and I know I have to do everything in my power to hang on to it. No matter the cost. "What time is it?" I ask as I get to my feet. "What day is it?"

"You've been trapped down there for six days," my sister says, wiping away her tears. "It's Monday morning, around seven."

"Then I still have time," I say with a faint smile.

"Time for what?" my mother asks.

"To make my court date."

"That's the last thing you need to be worried about," my father says as he takes my arm. "It's all been taken care of. Extenuating circumstances. Our lawyer got you out of it," he adds quietly.

I look up at him and shake my head rapidly. "But I don't want to get out of it."

"He doesn't know what he's saying," he says to the officer, before gripping on tighter. He whispers in my ear, "If you don't stay quiet, you're going to ruin your life."

"What about *their* lives?" I glance toward the jagged opening.

He looks at me incredulously. "They weren't real, son."

My jaw goes slack; I'm gulping down air, trying to find the words. "I *killed* them. Do you not understand that? I don't know what you got away with . . . how you sleep at night, but my life will be meaningless if I don't face this."

"*You* were the one who chose this," he says through clenched teeth. "Or have you *forgotten* that as well?"

"What . . . what are you saying?" My eyes well up.

"That night, when you called me . . ."

And, like a bomb going off inside me, it all comes back. Every last painful detail.

With blood on my hands, I called my dad.

As I stood there, watching Shy die, my dad gave me the choice.

Call the police and face this, or call the lawyer to fix this.

"I chose wrong," I say as I back away, tears streaming down my face. "I chose wrong."

Even with the heavy burden of what I've done, it feels like a million pounds have been lifted from my shoulders.

"It may have been the rapture . . ." I say, raising my head to face them, to face the world. "But they were real to me. And I keep my promises.

"I remember everything."

ACKNOWLEDGMENTS

I owe a huge amount of gratitude to my fearless and passionate editor, Melissa Frain; my publisher, Kathleen Doherty; assistant editors Zohra Ashpari and Amy Stapp; art director Seth Lerner; and everyone else at Tor Teen for giving me the freedom to create without limitations. I realise what a gift that is, and I thank you.

My agent, Jaida Temperly, is a goddess. Thank you for your endless support and enthusiasm. I can't imagine a better partner. Same goes for everyone at New Leaf Literary—you rock.

To the amazing authors who offered their early support: Stephanie Kuehn, Kara Thomas, Jasmine Warga, Courtney Stevens, and Kelly Loy Gilbert, thank you! I'm such a fan of every single one of you. It means the world to me to have your names in my book.

Thanks to Erin Morgenstern and Adam Scott for that pivotal road trip to Virgina—ghost hunting, caves, driving me all around Richmond searching for the perfect Tavish estate—you're true partners in crime and art and food.

Much love to Rebecca Behrens, Libba Bray, Danielle Paige, and Bess Cozby—I wrote much of this book in your presence.

My pals: Gina Carey, Virginia Boecker, Melissa Gray, Heather Demitrios, Kate Scelsa, April Tuchholke, Alexis Bass, Veronica Rossi, Eric Smith, Jenn Marie Thorne, and Lee Kelly—love you guys.

And to my family: Maddie, Rahm, John, Joyce, Cristie, Ed, Ragen, Evan, and Honeypie—may you never get trapped in a cave.